The Oasis King

THE OASIS KING

THE OASIS CHRONICLES

MARK DAVID PULLEN

NEW YORK

LONDON • NASHVILLE • MELBOURNE • VANCOUVER

The Oasis King

The Oasis Chronicles

Published in New York, New York, by Morgan James Publishing. Morgan James is a trademark of Morgan James, LLC. www.MorganJamesPublishing.com

Proudly distributed by Ingram Publisher Services.

Publisher's Note: This novel is a work of fiction. Names, characters, places, and incidents are either products of the author's imagination or used fictitiously. All characters are fictional, and any similarity to people living or dead is purely coincidental.

A FREE ebook edition is available for you or a friend with the purchase of this print book.

CLEARLY SIGN YOUR NAME ABOVE

Instructions to claim your free ebook edition:
1. Visit MorganJamesBOGO.com
2. Sign your name CLEARLY in the space above
3. Complete the form and submit a photo of this entire page
4. You or your friend can download the ebook to your preferred device

ISBN 9781631959615 paperback
ISBN 9781631959622 ebook
Library of Congress Control Number: 2022937917

Cover Design by:
Rachel Lopez
www.r2cdesign.com

Interior Design by:
Christopher Kirk
www.GFSstudio.com

Morgan James is a proud partner of Habitat for Humanity Peninsula and Greater Williamsburg. Partners in building since 2006.

Get involved today! Visit MorganJamesPublishing.com/giving-back

CONTENTS

PROLOGUE:

FUGITIVES

Vex struggled to open his eyes. The threshold was a fantastic device—a small metallic disk no bigger than a coffee saucer that allowed its user to travel back and forth through time and dimensions. Admittedly, this jump had been a lot more violent than he remembered. Like being sucked through the porthole of an airplane midflight, his entire body had broken down atom by atom before being manifested as whole on the other side. Vex stared blankly through the dome of the Silverback before coming to his senses. He began to feel sick and left the cockpit, climbing down the outside of the iron giant for fresh air and solid ground. He blacked out on the way down.

He sat up in a puddle. Unsure how long he'd been asleep, he tried to piece together the flood of thoughts and memories beginning to overwhelm his brain. He remembered activating the device as the soldiers fought to break down the blast-resistant door and return him to captivity. Bruce had been the first through the door, and Vex remembered saluting him mockingly from the cockpit of the exoskeleton right before making the jump. It wouldn't be long before Bruce tried to find him. That, however, would be no easy task. *We did it, Tiny,* Vex thought. Then, all at once, he remembered the little being that helped him escape. *Tiny!*

Vex jumped to his feet and saw Tiny lying facedown in the puddle next to the exoskeleton. The brute had returned to the vault deep inside Tiny's mind and left the small creature almost entirely devoid of life and energy. Vex pulled Tiny's miniature-sized, blue body out of the puddle and rocked him back and forth. Although Vex felt no loyalty toward anyone, he had quickly taken a liking to the little blue fellow while they were together in captivity. When all the others had left him behind, Tiny was his saving grace. Vex shook Tiny gently.

"Wake up!" Vex said firmly. Tiny's pure black eyes fluttered open, then closed.

"Tiny cold. Tiny sleepy," Tiny sighed before passing out again. Vex exhaled a sigh of relief and looked up at his new surroundings for the first time since he arrived in the valley.

This exotic green landscape could not be further from what he'd expected. The fresh outside air sure beat the air inside his jail cell, so he wasn't complaining. Once Tiny got back on his feet, they could leave and go wherever they wanted. The atmosphere in the valley was rich with a lingering scent of lilac and pine that tickled Vex's nose, and the breeze carried the scent of incoming rain. Vex could see the storm looming over the mountains, moving toward them quickly. They needed shelter.

He stepped out of the puddle and glanced down. *It can't be,* Vex thought to himself. Upon further inspection, a chill ran up his spine. A giant three-toed footprint lay before him, collecting more water as the first ripples of raindrops broke the surface of the "puddle." *Oh, that's just wonderful,* Vex thought as a nightmarish roar echoed across the valley.

In a panic, Vex scaled the side of the Silverback to the cockpit and desperately tried to start it. But the onboard computer just flashed an alarm. The console strobed red and black as the system alerted him that the machine had overheated. *Error 1012, system too hot for operation. Please allow time for full cooling. Error 1012, system too hot for operation. Please allow time for full cooling.* Vex balled his fist and slammed it down on the navigation screen, causing it to go gray with static. *Well, it isn't going anywhere without me driving it,* he thought in frustration. He rejoined Tiny on the ground just as it started to rain.

Vex threw Tiny over his shoulder and ran for what seemed like hours in the torrent of rain and wind. Tiny stirred only occasionally. Vex was getting tired. He needed somewhere, anywhere, that could provide respite from the unrelenting rain and cold. The shelter of the trees beckoned to him from afar. Maybe there was a place among the pines that could be suitable, if only for the time being.

He sprinted across the field, leaving a well-trodden trail in the tall grass behind him. The trees provided some asylum from the downpour. However, the wind seemed to swell inside the forest. He had traded one evil for another. His pace slowed under the shelter of the tree's high branches. Adjusting Tiny on his shoulder, he paused to catch his breath. The pint-sized lifeform wasn't heavy—more like dead, awkward weight—but Vex started to feel the fatigue from carrying him. Vex removed his hat and wiped the sweat and rain from his bald, green head. His pointed ears picked up the sound of whispers in the trees, and a very uneasy feeling swelled inside him.

Out of nowhere, he caught sight of movement. He focused his deep purple eyes, but perhaps it was nothing. The heavy rain did an outstanding job of impairing his perfect vision as he fought the urge to run. He secured Tiny more tightly to his shoulder and pushed forward. The forest ended abruptly, and Vex found himself standing in a wide clearing.

An enormous, prehistoric tree stood before them, deeply rooted in the clearing, branches tickling the sky. It was easily the tallest tree in the woods, but it was the giant knothole in the mammoth tree's trunk that captured Vex's attention. *Home at last,* Vex thought. He bolted across the clearing to the shelter of its branches. He knew climbing the tree with Tiny over his shoulder would be quite challenging, but Vex discovered he couldn't even reach the tree's lowest branches. "Now what?" he asked aloud. He slumped down under the tree and carefully set Tiny next to him before he gave in to exhaustion and closed his eyes.

The sounds of grunts and bellows caused Vex to open his eyes. As he shook off the fog of sleep, he witnessed the brute in a dustup with a colossal brown bear. Tiny had apparently gathered the strength to once again make the metamorphosis into the giant, hulking monster. Vex referred to the blue titan, with its granite-like exterior of oversized muscles and an attitude to back them up, only as Rumble.

Rumble crashed against the bear with nearly unstoppable force. The bear gnashed its jaws and, with a mighty swipe from its front paw, left deep claw marks across Rumble's chest. Rumble recoiled only briefly before launching a giant closed fist to the side of the bear's head. The bear flew backward and shook off the blow. It lowered its head and charged Rumble, knocking him to the ground. The bear pinned the brute to the ground with all its weight, unleashing a deafening roar and locking its gaze on Vex. Vex felt the blood in his veins go cold.

The bear whipped its head around and sank its teeth deep into the meat of Rumble's shoulder muscle. Rumble kicked violently, and his deep, bellowing grunts turned to high-pitched squeals of pain. Vex recognized the signal of the conversion. Rumble retreated, leaving Tiny behind in his stead, ushering in the bear's victory.

"Vex, help Tiny," Tiny cried out. Out of nowhere, the bear lifted its weight off Tiny, aside from the one paw that kept him pinned to the ground.

"Take the runt and leave this place, Vex," the bear roared. Vex furrowed his brow. *Did the bear speak?*

"I did not stammer. Take the runt and leave now!" the bear roared again, blowing the hat from Vex's head.

"Tell me, bear. How do you know me?" Vex asked, visibly shaken.

"I am Adalbern of the Valley, and I know all. Nothing happens in this valley without my knowledge. I know how you came to trespass here, and I won't tell you again. Collect Tiny, and leave."

"Okay, okay. We're leaving. We only happened on this place by accident," Vex replied.

"Accident or not, you are not welcome here. You are to leave by sundown."

"And if we don't?" Vex asked defiantly.

"You are more than welcome to stay and find out, though I promise you this. Not even the great blue brute can protect you here. I will have my way, one way or another. You have until sundown." Adalbern lifted his paw from Tiny's chest and lumbered away.

Vex lifted Tiny from the ground and carried him through the forest back to the exact spot where they had arrived.

"We go now. Tiny ready," Tiny stated.

"Yes. We're leaving. We should never have come here in the first place." Vex pulled the threshold from his coat pocket and twisted it in his palm. The light on the threshold flickered the faintest shade of blue before it made a humming noise and went black again. Anxiously, Vex twisted it in his palm a second time, and again the light flickered, the threshold hummed, and then nothing. Clearly it was malfunctioning. Vex knew they were stranded.

Days turned into weeks inside the knothole of the great tree. Vex and Tiny worked diligently, taking turns to try to repair the threshold. Unfortunately, neither of them had any idea how it worked or what to repair. Vex kept a sharp eye out for the bear, or anything worse. In the days they'd been stuck in the valley, he encountered many strange and frightening creatures. One day, while scouting for an alternate route out of the valley, a great, lumbering thunder-lizard had chased him across the prairies. On another evening, he was attacked by a huge saber-toothed cat, to whom he lost an arm. Thankfully, it would grow back. Soon after that encounter, he got carried away by a giant bat, which he killed, taking a nasty fall to the ground in the process. He eventually decided it would be best to stay in the knothole at night.

Bickering among themselves started sooner than Vex expected. Bitterness toward their situation gripped their hearts, and even though they weren't angry with each other, there was no one else to take out their frustrations on. Then one day, the bear started coming to the clearing to sit and watch. Its ever-seeing eyes drove Vex slowly toward madness as it sat staring into the knothole day after day. Vex yearned to put this place behind him and the bear along with it.

Then another thought occurred to him: Why not stay and get rid of the bear? Yes, it was a perfect plan. No one knew they were here, and they could make this place their own. He would trap the bear, and he would kill it. He could leave the knothole in the early morning hours before the bear arrived in the clearing and return late in the afternoon after it had departed.

Vex spent the following weeks setting traps throughout the valley. The thought of a bear-skinned headdress enticed his mind every waking minute. Numerous creatures wandered into the traps and died, but no bear. Vex was growing impatient. Cabin fever was the name of the game, and Vex was losing.

One dark, foggy morning, Vex looked out over the clearing from his perch in the knothole, and the answer to all his troubles slapped him right in the face: a game trail. The bear came and went from the clearing every day, using the same path, and Vex could see his route. He threw on his coat and hat, slipped silently out of the hole, and dropped to the ground. The time had come to exact his revenge. That singular thought became an infected, festering wound in his mind.

He would ambush the bear and take the satisfaction for himself. The thought of dropping down on the bear and putting an end to it with his knife gave his green skin goosebumps.

The trail wound its way around the outskirts of a large swamp, and Vex picked the perfect tree overhanging the path to hide in. He sat in the branches for what seemed like hours, waiting impatiently for any sign of the bear. Then, when he couldn't stand it any longer, he heard the sound of something trudging its way through the brush and briars. Vex gripped his knife and took a deep breath. Adrenaline coursed through his body, and he could hear his heart racing. He prepared himself for the ambush, but disappointment soon overtook him. A man and his four dogs emerged from the brush, wandering around beneath him.

As Vex watched the man, rage filled his heart. Men were the reason they were in the valley in the first place.

Suddenly, the man addressed him from the ground.

"Oh, thank God! Can you point me in the direction out of here? I'm lost," the man shouted, waving his arms.

Vex gave no response.

CHAPTER 1

THE PACKAGE ARRIVES

None of them could have guessed where the package came from or who could have sent it. Furthermore, they had no way of knowing that simply opening the package would ignite a series of events that would take them on one of the most extraordinary adventures of their lives. But that's getting ahead of ourselves. So let's start at the beginning, shall we?

It was a cool, crisp afternoon at Grammy's house. That's what the boys called her—Grammy, or Gram for short. Every summer they were sent off for a few weeks to stay with Grammy on the farm. The boys considered it a mini-vacation because they rarely had any chores to keep up with, and as long as they stayed out of trouble, they had the run of the house and property. Except for the library, which doubled as Gram's study.

They sprawled out with books and games strewn around the room due to the weather that kept them inside and confined to the den. Dylan stretched his back and glanced toward the window, watching as the rain continued to pour down.

"This is lame," he said with a yawn.

"Yeah, way lame," Jack agreed.

"What's *lame* mean?" Tripp asked. Although he was relatively bright for being only ten, he still wasn't quite "hip" to some of the things Dylan and Jackson said or did. Even though Dylan was twelve and Jackson eleven, they still relished the idea that they were older and wiser and therefore superior to their youngest cousin.

"He doesn't know what *lame* means," Dylan said, laughing.

"What a baby," Jack added, even though he wasn't quite sure what it meant either.

Tripp got up to stretch his legs. As he gazed out the window, he found himself entranced, watching the raindrops splash against the window and drizzle their way down the glass. Aside from the rain, it was reasonably calm outside. But alas, with no wildlife to entertain his gaze, he rejoined his cousins on the rug.

"I'm getting hungry," Tripp said.

"Good call, Sport. I could eat too," Dylan replied. He was always calling the younger boys by some silly, childish nickname.

"Do you think Gram will let us have ice cream for lunch?" Jack asked.

"No way. But as long as it's not hot dogs, I'll be happy," Dylan replied. He despised hot dogs.

The boys wandered from the den of the old farmhouse into the kitchen, where they found Grammy already preparing their lunch. The entire room smelled of homemade chicken soup and fresh-baked bread. The aroma of the chicken slowly simmering in a broth of onions, celery, and carrots, accompanied by the rich buttery smell of the bread, made their mouths water.

"Have you boys made a mess in the den?" Grammy asked, without turning her gaze from the hot pot of soup. Gram was always cooking something special just for them; she used food to show the boys her love. She was an easygoing woman and made things fun, but if they stepped out of line even slightly, she wasn't afraid to play the disciplinarian.

"We have, but we're still playing," Dylan replied.

"That's fine. Please clean up when you're finished," Grammy answered.

Dylan washed his hands at the kitchen sink, and the two younger boys followed suit. Dylan handed Tripp the soap while Jack fixed his gaze elsewhere. Sitting on the counter, just beyond the sink, sat the cookie jar. He crept over to it and stood on his tiptoes as he quietly lifted off the lid and removed a cookie. Then he gingerly replaced the top and lifted the cookie to his mouth.

"No snacks before lunch, Jackson!" Grammy snapped. *How did she know? She didn't even turn around,* Jack thought, silently returning the cookie to the jar.

They all made their way to the table for lunch and ate hurriedly. When they had finished, they pushed in their chairs and placed their dishes in the sink before being dismissed.

Dylan and Jack went back to finishing their puzzle in the den while Tripp flopped on the couch and scrolled through the channels on the old black-and-white TV. None of the boys could understand how Gram could enjoy the modern marvel of cable TV on such a small, obsolete viewing instrument.

All was quiet in the house when the doorbell rang. The boys jumped as if some ghostly specter had reached out and touched the backs of their necks with cold, supernatural fingers.

"That got me!" Dylan said, laughing nervously. The boys shuffled into the foyer just in time to see Grammy accept a package and close the door. Tripp peered out the window next to the door and through the rain could just barely make out the postman climbing back into his truck.

Grammy headed back to the kitchen, where she placed the package on the table and greeted the boys with a smile.

"What's up, guys?" Gram asked, continuing to look through her stack of mail.

"What's in the package?" Dylan asked.

"There is no return address, but it's addressed to the three of you. We'll open it together after supper, okay?" a distracted Gram answered as she tore open a letter, retreated to her study, and closed the door.

Dylan lifted the package off the table and examined it.

"What do you suppose it is?" Jack asked. His birthday was right around the corner, and he assumed it could only be a gift for him.

"Probably something one of our parents sent us," Dylan replied. Tripp just shrugged and nodded in agreement. As Dylan examined the package further, he noticed it was addressed to the three of them and did not have a return label, as Gram had said.

PLEASE DELIVER TO:
Mr. Dylan Waxwell
Mr. Jackson Stackman
Mr. Tripp Fuller
47 County Route 15
Gilbury, New York 18582

Tripp snatched the package out of Dylan's hand, ran for the den, and with the older boys close behind, slammed the door shut. Then, without thoughts of getting in trouble or consequences, the boys tore open the package.

Beneath a mound of packing and paper, they found a pocketknife, a wooden slingshot, and a small lantern.

CHAPTER 2

CRIME AND PUNISHMENT

The boys each pulled out one individual item at a time. Dylan chose the pocketknife, and Jackson grabbed the slingshot, leaving the small lantern for Tripp. Tripp accidentally hit the button on the top of the lantern and turned it on. The light shone so brightly that it left the boys stunned for a moment.

"Hey, watch that!" Dylan shouted.

"Yeah! What are you trying to do, burn our eyes out?" Jack asked. Tripp just chuckled to himself and turned off the lantern, noticing a small golden placard that read "Light of the World" as he did so.

"What do you suppose these are for?" Jack asked.

"Gifts. Things we can use on our next adventure," Dylan replied.

"Mine is better than yours," Jack stated. Dylan just scowled.

While they argued, none of them noticed the door cracking open. Grammy slipped into the room and stood there with her arms folded.

"It seems that I can leave nothing within your reach without curiosity getting the better of you," she stated in a harsh tone. The boys knew right away; they had been caught. Immediately all three of them turned to face her apologetically.

"There's an old saying about young boys: When they're quiet, they're up to no good," Grammy continued. Dylan swallowed hard. Tripp began to sweat. Jack dropped to his knees and pleaded for forgiveness.

"Oh, please have mercy on us, Gram!" he cried out.

"Good heavens, Jackson. Get ahold of yourself!" Grammy said sternly. Jack stood up red-faced, feeling foolish, while Dylan just shook his head in embarrassment for his cousin.

"I blame myself for being so distracted that I left you with the temptation to peek inside the package. But unfortunately, you chose to act on it, so you must be punished accordingly. Come with me, the three of you!" Grammy opened the door and motioned for the boys to pass.

Their heads hung low as they walked in a straight line down the hallway. Grammy led them through the kitchen to the closed door of the study, where she produced a key and unlocked the door. One by one, they shuffled into the large, windowless room. Bookshelves lined three walls, showing countless titles about faraway lands, dinosaurs, and strange unexplained phenomena. Pictures of maps and animals from all over the world covered the wall behind them. A grand chandelier made from bone and antlers hung from the ceiling. In the middle of the room was a desk with an old blotter and a globe; Gram's Bible was sprawled open on the blotter.

Wow, I've never seen a room like this in all my life, Dylan thought. The other boys were having similar thoughts, never having been in the room either. Gram came in behind them and closed the door. The boys turned to her and noticed GENESIS 27:3, in all capital letters, inscribed on the back of the door.

"What's that supposed to mean?" Dylan blurted out. Grammy moved to her desk and flipped through the pages of her Bible.

"Now therefore take, I pray thee, thy weapons, thy quiver, and thy bow, and go out to the field, and take me some venison," Grammy read aloud. The boys were puzzled by the language.

"Huh?" Tripp asked. Grammy just smiled sadly.

"That was your father's favorite Bible verse, Tripp," she said. The boys' ears pricked up. They rarely heard talk of Tripp's father, Dylan and Jackson's uncle. Tripp never had the chance to meet his father, and his mother never spoke of him.

"Tell us more about him!" the boys chorused. Grammy's smile faded.

"It's quite a sad subject."

Grammy got up from her desk and moved to the bookshelf, where she pulled out a tattered green book and placed it on her desk.

"Martin was a biologist—a brilliant man and an avid outdoorsman." The boys rushed to the desk. The green book

9

was an old photo album filled with many newspaper clippings and pictures. One picture was Tripp's father as a young man with his rifle, standing over the biggest white-tailed deer any of them had ever seen. Another had him standing on a dock somewhere, with a monstrous fish strung up by its tail. The newspaper clippings were fascinating. One read, "Local biologist discovers new species of toad, deep in the Amazon wilderness."

"That's him, boys. Our dear Martin," Gram said.

"What happened to him, Gram?" Tripp asked curiously.

"No one knows, son. He went into the woods with his dogs one day and never came home. He just disappeared. The police searched for months, but no news ever came of him. The trail and the case went cold together." Grammy said. She wiped a tear from her cheek and closed the photo album.

"Now, each of you is to go to a corner and stand facing it. You couldn't be patient enough to open that package after supper, so you'll learn patience the hard way by waiting out the clock." Gram said firmly, wiping another tear from her cheek. The boys groaned in unison. They had hoped she'd forgotten about punishing them.

They all went to separate corners and faced the walls. Tripp chose the one closest to Grammy, so he could watch what she did from the corner of his eye. They stood silently for what seemed like an eternity before Grammy pushed away from her desk and walked over to the door.

"I hope you've all learned patience and long-suffering in your punishment." The boys stretched and wiggled away their stiffness as they left their corners and walked into the

10

hall. Grammy grabbed Dylan on his way out and spun him around. His tall, lanky frame almost gave way due to his body's sudden halt, but Gram caught him.

Grammy knelt down and looked Dylan in the eyes. "You're the oldest, young man. You know better. Be an example to them. Those dimples won't always save you," Grammy said and ran her fingers through Dylan's thick, blond hair. In fact, all three boys shared this singular genetic trait: a distinct set of dimples in their cheeks when they smiled. Grammy stood up straight and released Dylan to the hallway before closing the door in his face, but not before he noticed a banner strung above the bookshelf that read, "May your roots grow deep, and your tallest branches toward the stars."

CHAPTER 3

WISH UPON A STAR

As the day drew to a close and evening came creeping in, the boys ate, bathed, and were sent off to bed.

"What do you suppose he was like?" Tripp asked.

"Who?" Dylan asked.

"Martin—er, my dad," Tripp replied.

"I bet he was all manners, a no-nonsense sort of fella," Dylan answered boldly.

"I don't think that at all. I bet Martin was a ham, a crazy adventure seeker," Jack rebutted.

"I think he was the perfect combination of the two. Strong and smart, but also fun and loving. A man a boy could really look up to . . . " Tripp said, his voice trailing off. Jack and Dylan could sense the sadness in Tripp's voice. They imagined that having never met his father must be hard.

Dylan tried to think of ways to distract Tripp. He glanced over at the window.

"Hey, it stopped raining. I wonder if we can see any stars tonight," Dylan said as he rushed across the room, lifted the window, and peered out. "Wow, look at them all!" he said excitedly. That was all it took—Jack and Tripp joined him at the window faster than you could blink.

The boys looked out at the night sky, watching all the sparkling stars as they danced and shimmered from so far away. They did their best to name the constellations.

"That's the Big Dipper over there, and Orion right there . . . " Dylan said, pointing to the sky.

"That star looks like it's moving!" Jack said.

"That's a plane!" Tripp replied. The boys all had a good hard laugh, and the mood once again became carefree.

"What a night," Dylan said, gazing up peacefully.

"Yes, sir," Jack replied.

"Look, a falling star!" Tripp shouted. The other boys were equally excited, having never seen a falling star either.

Just then, the bedroom door opened.

"Well, that was quite the commotion," Grammy announced. "Let's go, boys, off to bed." A few clouds had gathered, and it had started to sprinkle. Grammy closed the window.

"We're not even tired," Jack said with a yawn.

"Not tired indeed," Grammy said gently with a smile.

"Hey Gram, guess what? We saw a falling star!" Tripp said.

"Oh, you did? Did you make a wish?"

"Yup, all three of us seen it with our own eyes. I didn't wish, though. That's kid stuff." Dylan said.

"Saw, Dylan," Grammy corrected.

"Saw what, Gram?" Dylan asked.

"You saw, not seen. Your uncle used to drive me crazy with grammar like that."

"What was he like?" Tripp asked.

"He was a smart and charming young man. He had a childlike sense of adventure, which pushed him to be an outdoorsman and explorer. From a very young age, I always encouraged all my children to wish on falling stars and believe in all sorts of things, both logical and unexplained. He never got too old for that sort of thing. Now then, let's settle down."

With each boy in bed, Grammy began her nightly ritual of smooches and head rubs. First, she tucked Dylan under the covers, tousled his long, shaggy hair, and swept it behind his ears before kissing his forehead. Then she pulled Jack's covers up over his shoulders and swept his bangs off his forehead before kissing it. His hair was always styled according to the latest trends, whereas Dylan's was kind of a mop. This year's style was longer bangs pushed up in the front. Finally, she tucked Tripp into a cocoon with his blanket and rubbed the peach fuzz of his buzzed hair before kissing his forehead.

"Pleasant dreams, boys," Grammy said as she headed for the door. "Prayers?"

"Yes, ma'am, we said 'em already. Dylan led us," Jack replied honestly.

"Hey Gram, what did that banner mean? The one about the branches and stars?" Dylan asked recalling the banner from the study.

"'May your roots grow deep and your tallest branches toward the stars.' It's something I used to say to your parents when they were your age. It means I hope your faith keeps you firmly planted on a strong foundation while you reach for your dreams. Now, sleep tight, my boys." Grammy turned off the bedroom light and closed the door.

A moment after Grammy's footfalls faded into the distance, a flood of light arose from Tripp's side of the room as he turned on his lantern and giggled. Then came another giggle, followed closely by another, as Jack and Dylan both sat up in bed.

"That lantern is perfect for our midnight snack runs," Dylan said quietly.

"Yes, yes," Jack added.

"Yup." That was all Tripp had to add.

"As for now, I say we get some rest. First one awake wakes the rest," Dylan said.

"Deal," the other boys added in unison.

"Good night, fellas," Dylan said, as Tripp turned off the lantern.

Soon the room was quiet again, and Tripp crept back to the window. Looking out at the clouded sky, Tripp wished with all his heart on that falling star.

"I wish I could've met him." He let out a sigh as he headed for his bed, and it wasn't long before he drifted off to sleep.

That night none of the boys slept soundly. They suffered from bad dreams, varying from Jackson's nightmare of a worldwide candy shortage to Dylan getting forced to eat hot dogs until he threw up. But Tripp's nightmare was so lifelike, he wondered if it had really happened.

He dreamed that he was the only one awake inside the house as a storm raged outside. The house shook with the thunder, and the room filled with blinding light at every flash of lightning. He stood at the window, watching the storm, and with one flash of light, he saw the reflection of a man standing behind him. He spun around, but then the room went black around him—pitch black. He held his hands out in front of him as he tried to feel his way across the room.

Again the lightning flashed. This time there was a shadow in the doorway. He rushed toward it before the room went black yet again. Then he heard footsteps as the figure crept its way down the stairs. The dream was so real that he broke out in a cold sweat in his bed as he slept. He felt for the banister with his fingers, but it wasn't there.

He remembered the feeling of falling, but he wasn't falling at all. He was floating. He floated down the stairs until he could see that the front door to the house was wide open. At the threshold, he was sucked through the doorway by a tempest wind. Outside, the storm was explosive, and Tripp grabbed for the porch railing before he was sucked away. The sky was orange, and a giant black hole was pulling everything in the barnyard toward it, casting it into infinity. A green-skinned man strolled out of the house and stepped down the stairs, tipping his hat to Tripp and winking with his purple eyes. The strange man danced through the storm as though it were not happening, right toward the black hole. He reached into his coat pocket and produced a small metallic disk, turning it over in the palm of his hand before throwing it into the black hole. Then a giant red dragon erupted from the black hole and set fire to the barnyard.

Tripp sat straight up in his bed and let out a shout. It was morning now, and Jack and Dylan were both awake and already dressed for the day.

"Easy, buddy. It was just a dream," Dylan said soothingly.

"You all right, sport?" Jack asked.

"That dream was so real," Tripp sighed, relieved to be awake.

"You can tell us all about it after breakfast. Gram made chocolate-chip pancakes and bacon. Better get up and get dressed before we eat it all!" Dylan shouted as he and Jack ran out of the room.

That was too real, Tripp thought. Then the smell of bacon wafted into the room, and his stomach took over. He rushed out of bed and down the stairs to join his family.

CHAPTER 4

SWEPT AWAY

Tripp arrived just as Grammy was bringing the bacon and pancakes to the table. He slipped into the dining room and took his place next to Jack. Gram filled the boys' glasses with orange juice and sat down in her chair at the head of the table. She had noticed that her youngest grandson arrived late but did not mention it.

After filling their plates, the boys reached for their silverware—and Gram cleared her throat. Obediently, they stopped and bowed their heads as Grammy blessed their meal.

"Oh, gracious Lord, for what we are about to receive, let us be completely grateful. Bless us this day, in thy name, amen." The boys echoed her amen and immediately began to wolf down their breakfast.

"Slow down, boys," Grammy said. The boys adjusted their pace and continued to eat without speaking.

"Dylan, what are your plans for today?" Grammy asked.

"Well, Gram, the sun's shining, so me and the guys is going to go out to the field, or maybe go build a fort in the woods."

"Are, Dylan," Grammy corrected.

"Are Dylan what, Gram?" Dylan asked.

"You and the boys *are* going outside," Grammy snapped.

"That's right, we are. I just said that," Dylan replied cluelessly. Grammy just shook her head.

They finished their breakfast and cleared the table. Jack scraped the food off the dishes while Dylan put the leftovers away and Tripp wiped down the table and chairs.

"Thank you for all your help, boys. You're free to go now. Be careful, have fun, watch out for one another, and be back in time for lunch. And keep an eye on the sky. We have more rain coming in today," Grammy said as the boys ran up the stairs to their room. They laced up their hiking boots and threw on their hooded sweatshirts. Jack grabbed his slingshot, and Dylan stuffed his knife deep into his pocket as Tripp packed his lantern into a small knapsack.

"It's daylight, bro. We won't be needing that," Dylan said.

"Hey, you never know," Tripp responded. "I need to stop by the kitchen. I'll meet you guys outside."

"See ya in a few," Jack shouted over his shoulder as he and Dylan flew down the stairs and out the front door.

A few minutes later, after making his bed and tidying up his side of the room, Tripp made his way to the kitchen, which was empty. Apparently his grandmother had moved

20

on to chores elsewhere in the house. *Jackpot!* Tripp thought. He immediately began filling his knapsack with snacks from the cupboard. Tripp packed a box of crackers, some chocolate-covered granola bars, and a tin of fruit candies—for Jackson, of course. He zipped up his bag and joined his cousins on the front porch.

Dylan and Jack were already preoccupied with something at the corner of the porch.

"What's up, fellas? Are we ready to go?" Tripp got no response from his cousins.

"Hello?" Tripp asked sarcastically. Still no response.

"Hey, you two, what's going on?" he finally asked in frustration. He pushed his way past his cousins, and that's when he noticed a distinct set of boot prints in the fresh mud, next to the rosebushes.

"It's just like my dream!" Tripp gasped aloud.

"The dream from this morning?" Dylan asked.

"Yes, I dreamed there was a man on the porch. I couldn't see his face, but he was standing right here."

"Curious coincidence," Jack replied, unconvinced.

"Maybe, but this requires further investigation," Dylan said authoritatively, trying his best to sound like a detective. "Now that I'm looking, someone has been here and gone. That someone left a trail in the wet grass," he added, pointing. His cousins looked, and sure enough, a trail of trodden grass led away from the house.

"We should tell Gram," Jack said.

"Nonsense, we are men, and as such, we must protect her," Dylan stated, puffing up his chest and stepping off the porch. The other boys reluctantly followed suit. They followed the trail to the edge of the woods, where it became a little more challenging to follow with the mounds of leaves and fallen pine needles from the previous day's rain.

Once inside the woods, they found that the wind from the storm had cleared some of the debris from the forest floor, leaving it bare in some places.

"Over here—he went this way!" Jack shouted. He had managed to find a singular boot print in the mud.

"Excellent job," Tripp said.

"Thank you, sir," Jack said with a bow.

"Enough of the funny business," said Dylan, irritated. "We're on a mission."

They moved on, scouring the ground for any sign of disturbance. Being young men in search of adventure, none of them considered the danger they could actually be in. Although they believed they were giving chase, they hadn't considered that they could still be seen by prying eyes from afar. Or that maybe the trail was left on purpose, and instead of pursuing this stranger, the stranger was leading them straight to him.

They wandered through the woods, finding stray clues here and there along their path. By now the tall branches of the trees almost completely blocked out the sun.

"Is it me, or has it gotten dark out here?" Jack asked.

"And kind of creepy too," Tripp added.

"We should probably head back now anyhow. We don't want to stray too far from the barnyard," Dylan replied.

"Good idea. I'm kind of hungry," Jack said.

"We only ate a little while ago!" Dylan said harshly.

"I'm a growing boy!" Jack argued.

"Hey, you two hush for a second. I hear something," Tripp said softly. The boys grew quiet and listened intently.

"What is it?" Dylan whispered, tiptoeing closer to Tripp.

"I don't know," Tripp whispered. The soft sound finally reached Dylan's ears.

"That's water," Dylan replied.

After clearing their way through a small mound of brush, the boys found the source of the noise. The sound was echoing from the mouth of a tiny cave, and just inside the cave was another singular boot print. Not sure what to do next, Dylan and Jack just stood in silence. Tripp, however, dropped his small bag to the ground and began to rummage through it before pulling out his lantern.

"You're not actually thinking about going in there?" Jack asked.

"Why not? We have light," Tripp responded.

"You're out of your gourd," Dylan stated frankly.

"We should go back," Jack said.

"I'm going in, and you guys can't stop me." Tripp ventured into the cave.

Just then, a strange bird erupted from the cave and began flapping about madly as it was startled from its nest. This bird had brilliant blue plumage and flowing yellow tail feathers, the likes of which the boys had never seen. Jack shrieked, and Dylan covered his face, but Tripp just shrugged it off and went into the cave. Dylan's pride compelled him to follow Tripp. How could he stay behind while his youngest cousin went in? Jack, of course, followed suit, to prove he was just as courageous as they were.

Tripp's lantern not only did a fantastic job lighting their path, it also illuminated the entire area around them. They had to crouch at first, but soon the whole area opened up around them.

"This isn't so bad. I like it in here," Jack said aloud.

"Me too. It's kind of cool," Dylan added. Tripp was hyper-focused; the sound of rushing water was getting closer, and he wanted to find its source. The occasional bat fluttering from its perch was enough to send Jack into a panic, but Dylan just told him to relax.

They came to a slight bend in the tunnel, and the sound became a roar.

"We're close now. It must be on the other side," Tripp shouted.

"We can take a look. Then we head back!" Dylan called out. As they crept around the bend, Jack lost his footing and grabbed hold of Dylan, who then fell forward on top of Tripp. Before long, all three of them were rolling down the slope and crashing into the water.

Swept away in the water rushing through the underground cavern, they had discovered the source of the noise and now deeply regretted it. The water moved quickly and continuously bounced them around. Luckily, they had the sense to hold on to one another as they fell into the water. Occasionally pulled under, the boys started to gasp for air, choking and spitting up water as they were dragged further and further from safety. Finally, there was a flash of blinding light, and a new feeling arose inside them. The water disappeared, and they felt weightless. The hard bedrock underneath the raging water had come to an abrupt end, and they were falling now. The boys plummeted downward before crashing hard into the pool below.

They came up gasping for air and crying out for one another.

"Trippy, Jacko!" Dylan shouted in the darkness.

"I'm here!" Tripp shouted.

"Me too!" Jack cried. Assured they were all okay, the boys now faced the new dilemma of finding one another in the dark. A plopping sound echoed through the cavern, and a faint glow radiated from the bottom of the pool. Tripp's lantern had fallen from above and settled at the bottom.

Light of the world, indeed, Tripp thought.

"How lucky!" Dylan said aloud. He could now make out the silhouettes of his cousins against the darkness, and as luck would have it, they were not as far away as they had initially thought.

Once they were together and safely treading water, Dylan decided to dive down after the lantern. He took as deep a breath as he could and swam straight toward the bottom. The pool was quite deceiving in the dark. It seemed to go down for miles but was in truth relatively shallow, maybe ten feet deep. He grabbed the lantern, kicked his feet off the bottom, and swam for the surface. With the help of the lantern, it was only a few minutes before the boys were pulling themselves up onto land and wringing out their clothing. Tripp felt a chill run through his body as a cool breeze blew across his wet exterior.

"Hey, can you guys feel that?"

"That's a breeze!" Jack replied, holding his hand up.

"But where is it coming from?" Dylan asked.

"Probably deeper inside the cavern," Tripp replied.

"I don't think so. It's not musty like the air in here," Jack said.

"You're right. It's kind of sweet," Tripp said.

"And fresh," Dylan added.

The boys began to feel their way around the cavern. Tripp lifted his lantern as high as his arm could reach, and the boys scoured every wall of the cavern, high and low, searching for the origin of the breeze.

"There!" Dylan shouted, pointing toward a small hole of light in the distance. "That must be it!"

The boys walked toward the light and soon found themselves stepping out into the sunshine, where the warm air and cool morning breeze kissed their dirty faces.

FAR FROM HOME

As they waited for their eyes to adjust to the sunlight, the boys were finally able to breathe deeply in the warm glow of the late morning sunshine.

When he could finally get a good look at his surroundings, Dylan realized that the underground river must have carried them farther from home than they thought. The boys stood on a cliff face at the cavern's mouth that overlooked a vast, open valley. In the middle of the valley was a wide lake shimmering with the morning sun's rays, encircled by a large ring of trees. Surrounding that ring were expansive prairies with tall grasses of every shade of green and yellow waving to the boys, beckoning them for a morning stroll. Beyond the prairies were lush, green forests, alive with the morning breeze, and encircling the forests was a rolling range of snow-capped mountains, isolating the valley completely from the outside world.

"What a view!" Tripp said.

"Yeah, but something's wrong. None of this looks familiar to me," Dylan stated.

"Maybe we've never been this far into the woods before," Jack said with uncertainty.

"We're lost, right?" Tripp asked. His cousins nodded their heads in agreement.

"Well, we can't go back the way we came, so we have to climb down. Right?" Tripp asked.

"Then what?" Jack asked.

"Then we work on finding our way home," Tripp answered. The boys looked around for a minute in hopes that another answer to their particular problem might present itself, but they came up with nothing.

"Right, so down it is," Jack remarked.

As the boys began looking for a way down the cliff, Jack found a small, narrow footpath that wound its way down the hillside slope.

"Look over here—I found a path! Thank you, Jesus!" Jack shrieked.

"Amen, brother!" Dylan said, laughing.

"Before we go any farther, who wants a snack?" Tripp asked. All three of the boys had worked up quite an appetite. Tripp opened up his knapsack and began pulling out the various treats he had packed from Grammy's cabinets. The crackers were crushed, and the granola bars were a little soggy but still good. He only realized this as he withdrew a gooey, chocolate-covered hand from his bag. *Yuck,* Tripp thought. The only thing that wasn't damaged was the small tin of candies he had packed for Jack.

"I packed these just for you, but it looks like we're sharing," Tripp laughed.

"That's okay. It's the thought that counts," Jack replied lovingly.

The boy's conversation came to an abrupt end when a small nearby bush began to shake violently, and a strange yellow lizard emerged and scurried toward them. Lizards don't typically startle young boys, but this particular lizard did, only because the boys noticed it had six legs. Seconds later, a bird the size of a gull fluttered out of the bush and began pecking at the lizard. It was the same bird that had startled them before when they tried to enter the cave. The bird looked up at the boys and tilted its head before snatching up the lizard in its beak and flying away. They watched as the bird flew off toward the lake until they couldn't see it anymore.

"What just happened?" Dylan asked.

"That weird bird just ate that weird lizard," Jack replied nonchalantly, stuffing more candies into his mouth.

"I know what happened: The weird yellow . . . but the bird . . . six legs?" Dylan stammered, running his hand through his thick blond hair.

"I think it's a good idea to finish our snacks and start looking for a way back to the farm. It's getting a little too weird out here for me," Tripp added nervously.

The boys filled their bellies hurriedly and silently in the sunlight, when yet again their conversation was interrupted by an even stranger, thunderous sound. A deep guttural roar rose from the forest below. The boys jumped to their feet immediately, watching for any sign of what could have possibly made the sound.

"Look, over there!" Dylan shouted. The other boys already had their eyes fixed on their target. A man was running across a clearing below them at full speed toward a large stump on the clearing's far side.

"What's he doing?" Tripp asked.

"He's certainly in a hurry, that's for sure," Dylan said when another roar filled the air. This roar was much closer, and many of the forest's native birds left their nests in the trees' high branches and took to the air in fright. By that time, the man had reached the large stump and disappeared behind it. The boys could only watch as the following series of events unfolded.

The man was being pursued, but by what the boys could not explain. Then the great beast stepped out of the shadow of the forest and into the clearing. It was a thunder lizard, a giant red behemoth lumbering on two legs. Its huge claws hung low on long, swinging arms. The beast let out another roar as it searched the clearing for the man. It lowered its head to the ground to sniff the dirt as it moved forward slowly, scanning for movement with its slender yellow eyes.

The man bounded from his hiding spot behind the stump and let out a war cry, issuing a challenge to his pursuer. The thunder lizard stopped in its tracks, gave a lesser roar, and once more lowered its head to the ground, all the while keeping its eyes fixed on the man. Then the creature lunged forward at breakneck speed. It opened its jaws and dove for the stump. But the man was swift and leaped from the stump, grasping the beast by the horn on its nose. The beast stood up tall and yanked its head toward the sky, sweeping the man up into the air.

With one arm, the man held tight to the creature's nose, and with his free hand, he produced a great knife and drove it straight down through the beast's nostril and into the roof of its mouth. The beast let out a hideous shriek and began shaking its head violently to free itself from the knife. The creature shook its head so violently that it lost its balance. It fell on its side, kicking a cloud of dust into the air, and the boys lost sight of everything in the clearing. All they could do was listen to the crashes and bellows from their high perch on the hillside. Finally, once more a great yell rang out followed by a softer roar, and then the entire valley fell silent.

The boys waited for some time in the eerie silence as the dust settled. At last they could see that the man had emerged victorious. He arrogantly strutted around the downed creature. There was no denying that his victory was great.

He stepped toward the beast once more and sheathed his knife to his side when suddenly the creature's mouth opened wide and snatched the man up by the arm. It wasn't dead after all. It clutched the man with its powerful jaws and stood up, shaking him in its mouth. The boys watched in horror as the man was tossed around helplessly like a rag doll in the grip of the mighty beast's mouth. The creature threw its head back, tossed the man into the air, and opened its mouth wide to catch him. With the wildest streak of luck, the man bounced off the creature's gums and plummeted to the ground. With adrenaline surging through his veins, the man staggered to his feet and ran straight toward the forest. The creature growled deeply and gnashed its jaws before running after him, presumably to finish him off for good.

The boys were aghast.

"This is a dream. Wake up, Tripp," Tripp said, pinching himself.

"This isn't a dream. We're all awake," Dylan said.

"How do you know we're all awake?" Tripp argued. Dylan reached out and pinched him on the arm.

"Ouch!" Tripp shouted as he pinched Dylan back.

"Ouch! See, we're awake," Dylan replied, recoiling.

"That must mean we're dead!" Jack cried.

"Get it together, Jack. We still need to find a way home," Dylan snapped.

"If that's even possible."

"It's possible, Jack. We just need to get moving," Tripp said.

"Suggestions?" Dylan asked.

"There's still only one way to go—down," Tripp replied.

"Okay, then what?" Dylan asked again.

"Well, that man may need our help, and he may know a way out of here," said Tripp.

"Are you crazy?" Dylan argued. "That thing or something worse could still be out there. We don't even know where he went. We're not going after him."

"I'm listening if you have any other ideas," Tripp countered, "but so far, we know there's at least one other person here, and he may be able to help us." His logic was undeniable.

"Fine. All in favor of going after the stranger, raise your hand," Dylan said. Tripp and Jack both raised their hands.

"Okay, into the forest then," Dylan said with uncertainty.

They began to snake their way down the hillside. It took a few hours, but they eventually reached the bottom. The trees in the valley were much taller than the ones back home. They were almost intimidating. The boys gained their bearings and moved through the forest, occasionally stopping to look toward the cliff face to orient themselves. The distance to the clearing where the battle had taken place was much shorter than they expected. The clearing was a gruesome sight. Footprints and tracks here, vegetation crushed there, and mounds of dirt kicked up all over the place, accompanied by small pools of blood from the knife wound on the creature's nose. Seeing the tracks leading into the forest prompted Dylan's heart to sink further into uncertainty.

"Here we go, boys," said Dylan. "The real start of our journey."

They needed a minute to regroup. The sun was directly overhead now, and the morning coolness had turned to nagging afternoon heat. The trail wound its way through the forest before stopping at the edge of a widespread thicket. At that point, the trail stopped, and the thunder lizard's tracks turned off in the opposite direction.

"That thing ate him, or he went in there," Jack deduced.

"Either way, we've hit a dead end," said Dylan. "Let's head back before we lose daylight."

"I don't think so," Tripp said. "I have a feeling we should press on."

Without another word, Tripp pushed his way into the briars and disappeared.

"Tripp, stop!" Dylan shouted.

"Come back!" Jack called after him. They heard no response. The older boys had no choice but to go in after him. They scraped and climbed their way through the thicket, and suddenly they heard a splash.

"Ah, crud!" they heard Tripp shout. Before they knew it, Dylan and Jack came crashing down the bank and into the cold, murky water beside him. They had fallen into the murkiest, smelliest swamp anyone had ever seen, a swamp filled with bugs and black water that went on for miles.

"Now what?" Dylan asked angrily.

"I'm cold and wet, and I just want to go home!" Jack said, tearing up.

"Me too, Jack. What now, fearless leader?" Dylan asked Tripp sarcastically.

"We can't go any farther," Jack added.

"Oh yes, we can, and that right there is our ride." Tripp pointed past his cousins to a small wooden raft with two paddles, staked to the bank.

RIPPLES FROM BELOW

"You have to be joking," Dylan remarked, as the boys stood staring at the raft.

"I kid you not," Tripp replied. He shoved his way past Dylan and climbed onto the small raft. It was really more of a primitive means of transportation than a raft. It was built from logs and bound with cordage that had deteriorated from the many seasons it had clearly spent sitting idly in the swamp. The most peculiar thing was the post that rose from the very front of the raft.

"There's no way we're getting on that thing," Dylan insisted.

"Then go back to the cliff," Tripp answered.

"Tripp, this isn't a game anymore!" Dylan shouted.

"Look, we search for adventure every time we go outside,

and now we have the chance at a real one, and you want to run home?" Tripp asked.

"This isn't about having an adventure," Dylan replied vehemently. "It's about getting home in one piece. Look, the farther we get from that cave, the farther we get from home." Whether he was right or wrong, Dylan made a strong argument. Jack began to sniffle and tear up again.

"Don't you worry, Jack. I'll get us home," Dylan responded. He turned to Tripp. "You do what you want, but we're going back."

While his cousins worked together to climb their way back up the muddy embankment, Tripp struggled alone to get the raft afloat. Then Jack caught movement out of the corner of his eye. The red behemoth had been stalking them. Jack let out a blood-chilling scream before grabbing Dylan and flinging the two of them back down the bank and into the water as the creature came crashing through the brush after them.

Tripp watched in horror as Dylan and Jack had no other choice but to swim toward the raft in the swamp's cold, murky water. They swam several yards to the raft, where Tripp waited to pull them aboard the small craft. Tripp hoisted his cousins onto the raft, and without another thought, he and Dylan grabbed the paddles and began to row as hard as they could for deeper water.

"Wait, it's not following us!" Jack exclaimed. The creature just stood there on the bank, leering at them. Then it let out a loud, shrill shriek and began madly stomping its feet before standing straight up and running off through the thicket.

"Looks like you're going to get your adventure," Dylan remarked.

"I'm just glad we're all together and safe," Tripp added.

"Let's just try and find our way out of this swamp," Dylan responded as he began paddling.

Bugs flew about the swamp in droves: tiny biting things that latched on, bit, and flew away, and giant buzzing beetles that sounded like airplanes as they flew past your ears.

"I'm sick of this place already," Dylan said aloud. Strange skeletal trees grew out of the marshy waters, misshapen and contorted as they grew upward with little to no leaves or branches. The ones that did have branches were home to a variety of strange-looking nests.

"I've never seen a nest like that before," Jack said.

"I don't think we've seen how strange this place really is yet," Dylan replied.

The boys had rowed for what seemed like hours when they happened upon a large tree growing out of the water. This tree had an arrow carved into its trunk, pointing in the direction the boys were traveling. Next to the arrow grew a singular, small, narrow branch with a nest on it, and the strange blue bird from the cliff and the cave fluttered down and landed in the nest.

"That's weird," Tripp said.

"It's that bird again," Jack added.

"Should we keep going this way?" Dylan asked. Jack noticed a school of tiny baitfish breaking the water's surface, and a little way beyond them, bubbles rose from the deep. Then, finally, the bubbles burst at the surface, and a dense fog crept in and enveloped the small raft.

"This is starting to creep me out," Jack said.

"Me too," said Tripp.

"Why don't you hang your lantern from that post up there?" Dylan suggested. Tripp reached into his bag and hung his lantern from the post at the front of the raft, and it did a marvelous job breaking through the fog.

Once again, Jack noticed something in the water. Tiny blurs of blue light whizzed around the boat in the water. Jack cupped his hands and scooped up one of the lights to find a tiny glowing baitfish.

"Hey, check this out!" Jack shouted, showing his cousins.

"Turn off the lantern," Dylan told Tripp. With the light from the lantern extinguished, the boys watched as the school of tiny glowing baitfish danced around the boat, circling here and there before scattering in different directions, like the eruption of fireworks. Then they felt a bump.

"What was that?" Jack asked.

"I don't know—I can't see anything in this fog," Dylan replied. Once again, something underneath them bumped the raft.

"Stop paddling!" Dylan commanded. The raft sat quietly adrift in the water in a deafening silence.

Suddenly the raft began to move by itself as though in a wake of terror. Something beneath the raft was carrying it across the surface of the water at an uncontrollable speed. The boys cried out and hung on for dear life. Then whatever was under the raft stopped moving, and the small craft was propelled forward on a wave before coming to an abrupt stop as it crashed against the bank.

"Everyone away from the water!" Tripp shouted as he struggled to get to his feet.

The boys rushed from the water's edge as quickly as they could. As if they hadn't already felt lost, now they felt utterly helpless with the raft in pieces and no way back across the great swamp's dark water. The boys watched as the thing that propelled the raft emerged from the depths and climbed its way onto the bank. It was a giant amphibian—a devil frog, if you will. It was perfectly camouflaged with black and brown spots all along its sleek green body, undoubtedly the apex predator in the swamp.

The huge frog opened its mouth and revealed row upon row of sharp, jagged teeth. The boys could hear its labored breathing as it hauled its enormous body onto shore. Then, with one swift motion from its powerful hind legs, the frog lifted itself into the air and crashed down just feet in front of them. All three boys froze. They hoped that by remaining completely still, maybe the creature wouldn't see them. But in reality, the boys couldn't have moved even if they'd wanted to.

Then the frog opened its mouth once more and sent its tongue flying. It struck Dylan in the leg and stuck with its glue-like saliva. The creature started to drag Dylan toward the water as it backed its way off the bank.

"Help me!" Dylan screamed. Tripp and Jack grabbed Dylan by the arms and began to pull, but the frog just pulled them along with him. Dylan could feel the cold water on his skin as the frog had managed to drag him back to the water's edge. There wasn't much time left. Dylan knew his time had come.

"Take care of Tripp!" Dylan said, looking deep into Jack's eyes. Jack released his grip, thrust his hand into Dylan's pocket, and produced his new pocketknife. He began to cut away at the frog's tongue. But the tongue was so rough and the saliva so sticky that they dulled the knife's blade, and it stuck to the creature's tongue before it could do any actual cutting.

All hope seemed lost. But there were more powerful forces at work inside that swamp that day, and little did the boys know, help was already on its way.

Where they came from, the boys had no idea, but the warriors arrived in near perfect time. The sound of their barks and their commanding presence were enough to get the frog to release its grip on Dylan and drive it back to the deep waters of the swamp. Jack and Tripp dragged Dylan back up onto the bank, and the dogs came forward to lick the wounds on his leg.

THE HOLLOW

The boys were aghast. Dogs, here? *If there are dogs here,* Dylan thought, *there must be other people, and other people means a way home.* The dogs ran in a small circle on the shore, playing and delighting in their victory over the monstrous amphibian.

There were two males and two females, each of different breeds: a female black lab, a male golden retriever, a female mutt with beautiful black-and-brown fur, and the smallest dog in the group, a black-and-white basset hound, also a male. They were clearly working dogs but were well kept and maintained with gorgeous leather collars.

The dogs jumped and licked at the boys' faces until all three were giddy with delight. The mood had lightened for the moment.

"They're all so friendly!" Jack laughed. He picked up a stick and threw it as far as he could. The dogs raced after it, and shortly after that, they all returned carrying four different sticks and dropped them at Jack's feet.

Jack bent down once more and grabbed a stick to throw when the hound pricked up his ears and raised his nose to the air. He let out a long howl and waddled back in the direction he and the other dogs had come. One by one, the other dogs fell in line behind him and continued on their way. Finally, the hound turned to the boys and let out a sharp bark.

"Where ya going?" Dylan asked. The hound barked twice more at them and made off after the other dogs.

"Hey, wait for us!" Tripp shouted, chasing after the dogs.

"I wish he would stop running off like that," Jack said to Dylan, as they ran after Tripp.

Occasionally the hound would lower his nose to the ground and then signal to the other dogs by barking to get them back on course. Eventually, they made their way out of the marshes surrounding the swamp and into a wide area where the ground was hard, rocky, and devoid of vegetation.

Strange clusters of tall mushrooms grew in bunches as far as the eye could see, and a low-hanging mist hugged the ground and enveloped the boys' feet.

"This place gives me the willies," Jack whispered.

"Me too," Tripp replied. "On the bright side, we have the dogs to protect us now." Sounds of snarls echoed through the hollow, tickling at the boys' ears and imaginations. Then, all fell silent again.

"What do you think that was?" Dylan asked.

"I don't know, but I don't like it," Tripp replied.

"And I would rather not find out," Jack added.

The dogs continued to move forward silently as they followed the hound and his nose. Nothing seemed to sway or distract them from their course.

"They're moving like they want to get out of here just as badly as we do," Jack remarked.

"Good," Dylan replied. That means we have to keep up, and soon enough, this place will be behind us."

Suddenly a loud, echoing squeal erupted from the silence as a strange wild pig came barreling through the fog toward them. Jack let an equally loud, alarming squeal, which sent the pig in the other direction in a fright.

"Way to go, Jack!" said Dylan, surprised. "You scared it away."

"Thanks—just doing my part to keep us safe," Jack said proudly, not mentioning that he hadn't meant to scare the pig but was just reacting in fright.

Dozens of crows were perched overhead, watching them snake their way through the hollow's maze. The boys could feel their eyes on them, watching their every move from atop the giant mushrooms.

"The swamp was not such a bad place compared to this," Dylan remarked. The farther they went into the hollow, the more aware the boys became of a high-pitched humming in their ears.

"What's that sound?" Tripp asked.

"I'm not sure," Dylan answered. "I heard it the minute we stepped into this awful area of the valley." The sound grew louder and louder as they followed the dogs deeper into the hollow. A humdrum feeling washed over the boys the longer they lingered in this place.

"I don't want to go any farther," Jack said.

"Me either," Tripp replied.

"I don't see why we have to," Dylan agreed. "Let's just sit for a while." The boys huddled together under a mushroom and plopped down on the ground. Their will to get out of the hollow was getting sucked away with every step they took. The gloom in this place was so heavy and depressing that it sapped the boys' desire to go on. The dogs, sensing trouble, tried to nuzzle them to their feet, but they couldn't coax the boys up.

The fog all around the boys began to stir as some kind of faceless threat started closing in on them. In their mundane trance, the boys were sitting ducks. Then the ground beneath them began to crumble and mound as the first of the giant centipedes poked its antennae through. Mound after mound appeared as dozens of centipedes, some as long as three feet, worked their way to the surface toward the unsuspecting boys.

The dogs started snapping at the giant subterranean insects, clamping down on their exposed parts, but their numbers were great. The defensive circle the dogs had set around the boys grew tighter and tighter as the insects pushed them back. For every centipede that retreated to its hole, wounded, it seemed more were surfacing to take its place. But the dogs continued to fight despite the overwhelming odds.

The hound howled, and the other dogs barked and bayed viciously, but the centipedes were relentless. The first wave had now broken the dogs' perimeter around the boys and began feeling them out, deciding the softest, tastiest place to start munching. The mutt grabbed a centipede around its trunk and clamped her jaws shut, pulling it away from Dylan's face. She shook the centipede in her mouth so violently that it broke in two, freeing the boy.

The high-pitched hum suddenly grew louder as it echoed throughout the hollow, and the boys had to cover their ears. Then, snapping out of their trance, they took witness of the struggle happening all around them. Pushing the centipedes away where they could, the boys joined the dogs' fight. Jack launched rock after rock from his slingshot, but most of the shots missed, the dogs bit and snapped away at them, and Dylan and Tripp kicked at every insect that tried to surface from its hole. At last, they were able to push the centipedes back when the high-pitched hum resounded once more, this time sending the centipedes back underground.

"We did it!" Dylan shouted.

"Way to go, guys!" Jack said.

"And dogs!" Tripp added.

The dogs wasted no time and darted away from the wicked place where the centipedes dwell. As the boys gave chase, the high-pitched humming got louder and louder.

"What *is* that?" Dylan asked impatiently. Just then, the fog parted, and there before them was a massive silk cocoon the size of a city bus. Several of the centipedes were trying to burrow their way inside the cocoon. A strange sense of pity washed over the boys, and the desire to help the vulnerable creature inside propelled them into action. The boys chased the centipedes back to their holes, and the high-pitched hum rang out in their ears before ending abruptly.

"What do you think is in there?" Tripp asked. He strolled forward and placed his hands on the soft exterior of the cocoon. He could feel the gigantic organism inside stir as its racing heartbeat reverberated through the palm of his hand and up his arm. The silk and fibers of the cocoon had a rough, wool-like texture against his soft skin. Suddenly, the high-pitched hum echoed out from the cocoon again. The creature inside was crying out, and the cocoon started to shake and wiggle violently. Something unexplainable stirred inside the boys. Perhaps it was because they could relate to the gargantuan creature inside the cocoon, whatever it was, because they too felt alone, helpless, and vulnerable.

All three boys instinctively placed their hands on the cocoon in hopes of soothing the transitioning creature inside. Unbelievably, it worked. The boys could feel the beast inside the cocoon relax every tensed muscle in its body.

"What happened?" Jack whispered.

"I don't know. It was struggling, and then it stopped." Dylan replied.

"It's sleeping," Tripp said finally. The labored heartbeat and breathing had mellowed into a quiet rhythmic tone as the beast returned to its slumber.

CHAPTER 8

JOURNAL ENTRY 3600

I am lucky to be alive to write these words. Even after all these years, this place perplexes me. The environment remains hostile, and its inhabitants are truly savage.

Today I ran for my life as a red behemoth pursued me. My mind raced, and I remember thinking, I need Tiny. But Tiny was at home, back in the clearing.

I raced through the thicket toward the great tree, with the beast on my heels. I could feel its eyes on me and its hot, stinking breath on my neck. My pace was slowing.

As I ran, I sought any sort of cover. Some hole or crevice to climb into and wait the beast out. But there was nothing. Like an open wound, I was exposed to the beast and its will. It pursued me to the edge of the swamp, where the great amphibian lives.

I knew not to disturb the water, lest I drew its attention as well. I needed a distraction.

By the time I noticed the root, it was far too late. It hooked around my foot, and before I knew it, I was falling face-first to the ground. My wounded arm buckled under my weight, and I was unable to catch myself. I closed my eyes and waited to feel the pain of the behemoth's teeth as they closed around me for the last time. But the feeling never came.

Then I heard a familiar sound. Tiny had come to my rescue.

He had once again made the metamorphosis, and Rumble stood in his stead, gripping the behemoth by the tail. The creature was unable to come any farther with the weight of Rumble pulling against it, restraining it in place. With one swift yank, Rumble pulled the creature away from me, allowing me to get to my feet and safely away. The behemoth whipped its head around and gnashed its teeth at Rumble, but Rumble knew no fear. The creature was laid out with a swift closed-fist strike on the nose from Rumble, and it reeled in pain from the existing wound I inflicted with my knife. The behemoth roared and charged at Rumble, but he evaded the beast magnificently and kicked its feet out from underneath it—a true exhibition of his speed and strength.

But we were not alone. As I stood watching Rumble and the behemoth duke it out for my own personal well-being, I noticed a shadow moving through the water: the amphibian. The giant amphibian that calls that cursed swamp home had been attracted to the sounds of the struggle and was closing in.

This is it. This is our exit strategy.

"Rumble! Move it toward the water!" I shouted. And Rumble heeded my call.

Rumble led the behemoth toward the water and beckoned the creature to come for him. There was an explosion in the shallows as the amphibian presented itself. It roared from the water, and the behemoth answered its call with a roar of its own. But Rumble was stuck in the middle. The creatures crashed against each other on the bank with tempestuous force. Neither one relented, their violence only grew as they fought to secure their next meal.

The amphibian flicked its tongue, and the behemoth swiped at it with its giant claws. As the waters foamed around them, Rumble was barely able to escape the fray with his life. As the two titans wrestled in the shallows, we prepared to make our escape.

Then all went quiet. The behemoth and the amphibian had stopped brawling and now seemed to be listening intently. Something had attracted them, and they stood, waiting and listening. The amphibian ducked under the surface of the water and disappeared, as the behemoth lifted its nose to the air and sniffed. It let out a low growl before scaling the bank and disappearing into the swamp.

I don't know who or what produced the sound "Ah, crud!" But I'm sure they've been made a meal of by now.

"Ah, crud!" What could this possibly mean and what produced such a sound?

CHAPTER 9

SANCTUARY

The boys caught up with the dogs, who were sitting and waiting for them impatiently a short distance from the cocoon. Once the boys were in sight, the hound gave another sharp bark, and the dogs got to their feet and took off again. The hound led the small party on a direct path away from the hollow at a brisk pace. He was relentless in the pursuit of his invisible trail.

Soon the mushroom clusters and stalks shrank, and the ground took on a soft, mossy feeling under the boys' shoes.

"That's more like it," Dylan remarked. Even the dogs' pace had slowed, a sure sign to the boys that danger was not present at the moment.

"I hope they're taking us somewhere we can rest. I can't wait to get these wet shoes and socks off," Jack said.

"I know. I can already feel my feet starting to blister," Tripp replied.

"And I need to get a look at my leg," Dylan added.

All at once, the dogs disappeared into the bushes, and the boys followed. When they came through on the other side, they stood together in a rolling meadow filled with tall grasses waving in the breeze and patches of colorful wildflowers blossoming in the sun. The petals of some were vibrant purples and reds, while others were brilliant yellows with deep blue spots.

"What a strange and beautiful place," Tripp exclaimed.

"I wonder where they're taking us," Jack said.

"Hopefully somewhere warm and dry, with food," Dylan replied.

"Yeah, I could eat," Tripp agreed.

From its high peak in the afternoon sky, the sun began moving closer toward the horizon.

"We haven't even been here a full day yet, and we've already seen so much," Tripp said.

"After we get some sleep, we need to get back on track and figure out how to get home," Dylan remarked.

The dogs stopped abruptly on the trail in front of the boys. The mutt crouched down on her front legs, her hackles standing straight up. She bared her teeth and growled ferociously at a large patch of wildflowers growing on the side of the trail. This defensive action set the boys on edge. They huddled closer to the dogs and braced themselves for some strange, hungry beast to charge at them from the tall grass. But nothing happened.

"What's going on?" Jack whispered.

"I don't know, but I don't like it," Dylan said.

"They must've gotten wind of something," Tripp said.

Suddenly, the dogs began barking erratically, and the wildflower patch began to move and shake as a massive brown bear emerged from the bushes.

"A bear! Get him, dogs!" Jack shouted. The bear sniffed the dogs individually, and each immediately lay down and began to whimper. Then the bear turned its gaze to the boys.

"Nobody move," Dylan whispered, as he and the boys froze in place. The bear stared at them for quite some time, sniffing them out but not coming any closer. Then, finally, the bear slowly lumbered away in the opposite direction, followed closely by a rather large badger. As the badger scurried between his legs, Dylan was sure he heard someone say, "Pardon me; mind your feet, gents," but he shook it off. *Nah, there's no way*.

The dogs sat on the path, watching as the two animals walked off through the meadowlands together.

"What do you suppose that was all about?" Tripp asked.

"Such a strange pair of animals to be hanging around with each other," Jack added.

"This place keeps getting more and more strange," Dylan said. Once the two animals were out of sight, the dogs continued on their path, leading the boys toward the forest that now lay before them.

The dogs began jumping and barking excitedly before running straight into the trees. The boys chased after them as fast as possible, but they were no match for the dogs' natural speed. Plus, they were tired from the day's events and unable to keep up. The boys would have certainly lost their way had it not been for the dogs' wild barking. They had run only a short distance when they found themselves running out of the woods and onto a beach at the edge of the most pristine-looking lake they'd ever seen. The water sparkled in the sunlight, clear and still as glass.

"Now there's a sight for sore eyes," Dylan stated.

They caught sight of the dogs dashing along the beach toward a large rock formation on the far side of the lake. As the boys walked along the sandy shore, quite some distance behind the dogs, they did their best not to disturb the water. Based on their experience, they didn't want some great, hungry thing to make its way out of the water after them.

"Hey, why are we following these dogs anyway?" Jack asked.

"We didn't really have a choice. At least with the dogs, we should be safe," Tripp said.

The boys rounded the beach and observed the dogs climbing a narrow staircase cut into the side of the great rock. They followed the stairs to the entrance of a large cave, where the dogs had stopped. Then the dogs entered the cave.

"I guess this is going to be home for the time being," Dylan said. Just then, a tall, bearded man emerged from the shadows and stood at the mouth of the cave.

"This is our home, and by all means, come inside and make yourselves comfortable," the man said.

CHAPTER 10

SUPPER AND QUESTIONS

The man was tall and broad in stature, with shaggy brown hair and a bushy brown beard. The boys couldn't quite put their thumb on it, but there was something familiar about him.

"I see you boys have already met my furry family. They're a good bunch, but not much for conversation," the man joked. The boys were reluctant to speak and debated whether to run for their lives.

"I suppose if you're this talkative already, it makes no sense to ask where you came from, but I will most definitely take your company regardless," the man said, chuckling.

"Who are you?" Tripp blurted out.

"How amusing that of the three of you, you'd be the one to ask that question. My name is Martin, and I'm your dad,

Tripp." There was a deafening silence. Of all the things they had already experienced, this was indeed the strangest.

"Wait, what?" Jack asked.

"It's true, Jackson," Martin replied.

"How do you—"

"Know who you are?" Martin asked, clearly holding back some emotion. "It's simple. Look at those dimples and those huge ears. You're Elaine's boy, and Dylan's hair gave him away. My older sister, Annette, if you need further proof, was always something of a hippie," Martin said with a smile.

"There's no way. You can't be. Gram said you were dead," Dylan said. But Tripp couldn't control himself any longer.

"It's so good to see you!" Tripp shouted as he hugged Martin around the waist. Martin whisked Tripp into the air and squeezed him tightly, tears streaming down their faces.

"There's so much we have to talk about!" Tripp cried, holding on to his father.

"All in due time, son," Martin replied. "All in due time."

As Dylan watched Tripp and Martin together for the first time, he couldn't help but notice the uncanny resemblance. Sure, Martin had a beard and was more than a few years older, but Tripp was his spitting image. Still, he had some doubt.

How can we really know this is Martin? Dylan thought apprehensively.

The long-overdue hug lasted for several minutes. Neither Martin nor Tripp wanted to be the first to pull away. But when the embrace finally did end, Martin could tell Dylan still needed a little convincing.

"It's okay if you still have some doubts," Martin said, glancing at Dylan. "Take all the time you need to process this. But while I do my best to prove it to you, I have a question for you."

"Yeah? And what's that?" Dylan asked challengingly.

"Does my mother, your grandmother—forgive me, but I don't know what you call her," Martin admitted.

"Gram! We call her Gram!" Jack shouted.

"Thank you, Jack. Does Gram still watch cable with the old black-and-white TV in the den?" Martin asked.

Dylan's eyes widened, and he hesitated for a minute. *How could he know that?*

Jack, on the other hand, needed no more proof and was off and running with questions. "You *are* our uncle! Have you been here this whole time? Do you have anything to eat? Why do you have four dogs?"

"Whoa, whoa. One question at a time," Martin laughed.

"Sure. You must be as curious about us as we are about you," Dylan said with a scowl.

"Okay, you go first." Martin said.

"Food!" Jack shouted.

"That's not a question," Martin replied. But the other boys seemed to agree with Jack.

"You boys must have had quite a day. It was so long ago, but I remember my first day like it was yesterday . . ." Martin's voice trailed off. "Okay, so food it is," he finished.

Martin moved to a large circular pit and started a fire.

"I have no way to store food, so we tend to eat fresh every day. Most days, it's just fish and eggs because they're the easiest to come by, and not much goes to waste. So, you boys rest, and I'll be back in a bit with some supper."

Supper? Grammy always called dinner "supper." Maybe he is Grammy's boy, Dylan thought.

Martin grabbed a long spear with a sharpened stone for a tip and threw a small bag over his shoulder. He instructed the boys to stay inside in his absence and inspected the dogs, who now sat upright, waiting for their next task.

"Hmm. Okay, Nicholas, you can come with me. The rest of you know what to do while I'm gone." The boys looked at the dogs and then back up at Martin.

"Oh, how rude of me! Introductions: The hound is Toby, the mutt is Cinder, the black lab is Nicky, and the golden here is her brother, Nicholas. Not really her brother, but I bought them from the same kennel. All my dogs have specific jobs. I work, so they work. Toby, Cinder, and Nicky will look after you boys. Trust them. They know how to keep you safe here. Most importantly, boys. Do not, for any reason, go outside until I return." With that, he and Nicholas left the cave and disappeared down the steps.

The boys, left to themselves, wasted no time exploring their new quarters. The cave was less than extravagant. It consisted of a large open room with a large animal skin rug and a tiny wooden table. The fire pit in the middle of the room served as both heat and a stove, and at the rear of the cave was Martin's bed. A hole in the cave ceiling allowed light in and the smoke from the fire pit to escape.

"There's nothing to do here but play with silly old dogs," Jack whined. "I'm bored."

"You're bored already?" Dylan asked.

"Yup, bored. Let's go outside!" Jack exclaimed.

"Weren't you listening? We can't go outside."

"But I'm bored!" Jack whined. Dylan just scowled at Jack, and Jack huffed and puffed and plopped himself down on the floor.

Outside, the valley was beginning to come alive as the moon cast an eerie shade of blue light over the valley's entire landscape. A symphony of distant crows from nocturnal birds, the buzzing of insects drawn to the light from the fire, and the occasional growling of what sounded like large predatory cats echoed across the valley.

"This place is just primal," Dylan said as he looked out into the darkness. "It's unreal."

"It sure is," Tripp replied. Just then, a familiar roar echoed from the forest below as the red behemoth stepped out onto the beach and began lapping water from the lake.

"That's him!" Tripp shrieked. He crept to the edge of the rock and peered downward in hopes of getting a closer look at the beast.

"I thought I told you to stay inside!" Martin said as he came up the steps.

"Oh, Martin, I'm sorry. I heard that thing, and I just wanted to get a good look at it," Tripp replied.

Martin rested his spear against the wall and took the bag off his shoulder, while Nicholas came sauntering in behind him.

"I call her Lock-Jaw. Come with me," Martin said, gesturing. He led the boys down the stairs to the beach, where they watched the behemoth from a safe distance.

"She comes around here every once in a while to feed." Lock-Jaw waded into the water and disappeared beneath the surface. Her red scales twinkled ever so slightly in the moonlight as she swam and dove gracefully with serpentine motions. Finally, she emerged from the lake and climbed out onto the beach, where she sat and devoured a colossal fish of some kind.

"Did you see the way she moved? Wasn't it incredible?" Martin whispered. "And the way she eats—her teeth and jaws are like an anaconda's; her jaws expand around her food, and her teeth curve inward so nothing can escape when she clamps down on it."

"What is she?" Jack asked.

"I don't know—some sort of dinosaur maybe. She's magnificent. I know that much to be true."

Martin ushered the boys back up the steps and into the cave, where he emptied his bag of its contents and produced six decent-sized fish and a handful of wild eggs. He wasted no time preparing their supper by heating a large stone slab, cooking the eggs, and placing the fish on a makeshift rack over the fire.

"I wonder, though—if she's such a good swimmer, why she didn't follow us through the swamp?" Tripp said.

"That's where Goliath lives," Martin answered. "A massive beelzebufo. That thing eats anything that even goes near the water."

"What's a beelzebuffoid?" Jack asked.

"*Beelzebufo*. It means "devil frog," a giant prehistoric frog that ate dinosaurs. Why didn't you guys go around the swamp instead of through it?" Martin asked.

"We were following a man we saw," Dylan replied.

Martin and the dogs tensed up and bolted to the mouth of the cave.

"Tell me, boys. You saw another man?" Martin asked.

"Yes, a man in a gray coat," Dylan said. "You were telling us about Lock-Jaw's teeth. This guy almost lost his arm in a fight with her today."

"It will grow back," Martin whispered. "That wasn't a man. Of all the things in this valley, you boys watch out for him. He's a terrible, vile thing, and things always get messy when he comes poking around. I've managed to stay ahead of him for a while, but it's only a matter of time before we have another encounter. He's hunting me. He has this little blue goblin-looking thing that follows him around. Watch out for it too."

Martin moved back to the fire, removed their dinner, and set it out on individual clay plates. The boys were ravenous and began to shovel food into their mouths.

"I'll let it slide today, boys, but I usually thank God for my meals." The boys looked at each other with full jowls and hung their heads in shame. Then they all ate heartily, and when they had eaten their fill, they all took seats around the fire.

"Okay, question-and-answer time," Martin said.

"Where are we?" Dylan asked.

"This is an extraordinary place, boys. A long time ago, there was a great flood that swept over the earth."

"Noah's flood," Dylan interrupted.

"Yes, Noah's flood, exactly! So, since you already know the story of the flood, let me fast-forward. We serve a very merciful Creator, and this place is sort of like a second Eden. It's home to the creatures that weren't on the ark or that suffered from extinction shortly after that. My turn: how is everyone back home?"

"Mom and Dad are good. Dad just became a detective, and Mom dropped me off at Gram's on Monday because the contractors will be at the house all week," Jack stated.

"That's wonderful news! Your dad was still in the police academy when I . . . and your mom was super smart; she was applying to be a school administrator when I . . . uh . . ."

"When you disappeared," Tripp finished kindly. "I rode to Gram's with Jack and Aunt Elaine because Mom has to decorate her classroom all week, and then it's her annual girls' weekend with her college roommates. She never talks about you, though. Even when I ask. I think it still bothers her having you gone."

"I miss her so much. As much as I've missed you. I at least got to meet Dylan and Jack, although they were way too young to even remember me. Did she remarry?"

"Oh no. I'm far too much of a handful. Plus, I'm the only man she'll ever really need. We're doing just fine. We have a lot of ground to make up when we get home, though. She's a great mom, but terrible at man things. I get called names for the way she taught me to throw a baseball," Tripp said, trailing off.

"And we have to take care of the kids that call him names, if you catch my drift," Dylan added sharply. He cracked his knuckles and leered at Martin. *That a boy, Dyl. Stare him down. Show him you mean business if he wants trouble,* Dylan thought.

"You all go to the same school?" Martin asked, oblivious to Dylan's threat.

"Yes. Aunt Elaine and Aunt Annette moved home when I was about five. Mom and I needed some help, and everyone decided it made the most sense for the whole family to live closer together," Tripp replied.

"I am sorry it's been tough, Tripp," Martin sighed.

"What's for dessert?" Jack interrupted.

"I don't have anything for dessert," Martin said, chuckling.

After a pause, Dylan finally asked, "How do we get home?"

"I don't know," Martin replied.

The boys hung their heads. This wasn't the answer they'd hoped for, but it was the answer they expected. *It makes sense. If Martin knew how to get home, he would have left the valley a long time ago*, Dylan thought. Jack was sure everyone was probably already missing them and got a little emotional.

Instead of pushing the boys further into despair with more questions of his own, Martin decided it was time for bed. He stoked the fire and made sure the boys were warm as they stretched out on the rug. The dogs moved in and circled around them as they quickly drifted off to sleep. Martin covered them ever so gently with a blanket from his bed. Dylan felt Martin moving closer and peeked an eye open.

"Good night, boys. May your roots grow and your tallest branches toward the stars," he heard Martin say softly. Dylan sat up in his spot by the fire and looked Martin straight in the eye.

"I didn't mean to wake you," Martin whispered.

But Dylan was grinning. "It *is* you. Gram told us she used to say that to you."

"It is me, indeed. I'm so glad to have finally gotten to see the young man you've become, Dyl," Martin smiled. They embraced briefly, and finally feeling safe and secure in the cave, Dylan joined his cousins' slumber.

Martin sat up late at the table, deep in thought. "I ask for wisdom and guidance, dear Lord. I believe you've sent them for a reason. Help me to send them home safely when they've fulfilled their purpose." He made his way to his bed, and soon enough he, too, was fast asleep.

Martin awoke early the following day. The boys were sleeping soundly beside a dying fire, so he grabbed his bag and his spear and headed for the door. Toby got up and followed him to the cave entrance, where they stood together, taking in the view of the morning sun rising over the horizon and bringing the wild countryside to life along with it.

"Well, I suppose it's that time again, old friend." Martin knelt and patted Toby on the head.

"You're in charge while I'm away, got it?" Toby just sat panting and wagging his tail as Martin turned on his heels and headed down the steps.

Toby woke the other dogs, and they saw themselves out for relief. Then, after sniffing around the beach for a moment, they went to wake the boys. Cold noses on necks and licks on faces is not a welcome feeling in the morning, but it is an effective strategy, and the boys were soon awake and moving about the cave.

"How did you guys sleep?" Dylan asked.

"Like a rock," Tripp replied.

"Me too," said Jack. The boys searched for something to eat in Martin's absence, but alas, they found nothing.

"He was right about not storing food," Dylan concluded.

The boys strolled down the steps and stepped out onto the warm sand of the lake. Jack and Dylan fussed with the dogs, while Tripp decided to take a stroll down the beach. He was poking at the water and examining Lock-Jaw's footprints when he got a strange feeling that someone was watching him. He happened to look up and noticed someone standing just inside the trees. Thinking nothing of it, he took a few steps forward and waved.

"Martin, is that you?" Tripp shouted. But no reply came. The Stranger just motioned for him to come closer with a singular green finger.

"Hey, guys," Tripp shouted over his shoulder nervously. But his cousins and the dogs were too far away to hear him. Tripp took a few more steps forward, and the Stranger nodded and continued to beckon him forward with hand gestures. Tripp stopped several yards from the tree line and waited. The Stranger motioned to him again, but Tripp shook his head. The Stranger grunted at him and gestured to him more anxiously. His deep purple eyes pierced Tripp to the depths of his grieving soul. The Stranger snapped his finger and motioned Tripp closer, letting out an agitated sigh. But Tripp stayed in his place.

Finally, the Stranger rushed out onto the beach, grabbed Tripp by the arm, and dragged him toward the trees. The other boys heard his screams and cries for help, and they alerted the dogs, who bolted down the beach to help him. But before they could sink their teeth into the Stranger's flesh, a long, drawn-out howl from a calm and collected Toby turned the Stranger's courage to fear, and he released Tripp and disappeared among the trees.

The dogs stayed at the bottom step while Jack and Dylan ushered Tripp back to the cave.

"You okay?" Dylan asked.

"Yeah, what happened?" Jack added.

"I thought it was Martin. He just rushed out and grabbed me when I wouldn't go any closer. Did you see him?" Tripp asked as he massaged his bruised wrist.

"Scariest thing I ever saw," Dylan replied.

"That skin. Why was his skin green?" Jack asked.

"Martin did say he wasn't from here," Dylan said.

"You mean like an alien?" Jack asked.

"I need a minute, guys. I'm sorry," Tripp said, excusing himself from the conversation.

While his cousins sat and discussed the event, Tripp wandered into Martin's "bedroom" and began rummaging through his things. Martin had very few possessions. He had a large pack filled with animal traps, a camp ax, and a small leather wallet. There were also more spears like the one they had seen Martin carry, a cane fishing pole, and a lever-action 30-30 rifle. Tripp called the other boys to help him investigate his findings.

"Sure makes your slingshot and pocketknife look like toys," Tripp joked.

"I had a slingshot and a pocketknife when I was your age," Martin said from behind them, startling the boys. Tripp dropped Martin's bag and the wallet fell out.

"Be careful with that. It's important!" Martin said as he tucked the wallet into his pocket.

"Oh, sorry, Martin," Tripp said sheepishly.

"You're all a little jumpy, and what's with the dogs?" Martin asked.

"We had a little run-in with the green man." Dylan said.

"Where? He came here?" Martin asked.

"Yes, but we're okay. The dogs chased him away," Dylan replied.

"Well, as long as everyone is okay. You can explain it to me after breakfast," Martin said.

"More eggs and fish?" Jack asked.

"Eggs yes; fish no. Today is something of a special occasion, so we're going to celebrate our reunion. But first, come with me." Martin put his arms around the boys and ushered them to the mouth of the cave.

"I figure it's a new day, and after a restful night's sleep, I'd like to properly welcome you, my friends, to the Oasis!"

The morning sun was shining brilliantly on the crystal-clear lake of the Oasis, and the warm morning breeze carried the scents of lilacs, cedar, and pine. It was an experience the boys would remember for a very long time. Martin butchered a medium-sized wild pig and prepared it in the cave, along with the fresh eggs he had gathered. After cooking, he set the table, where he and the boys sat down, prayed, and enjoyed their meal. The whole clan ate well, even the dogs.

"Martin, can I ask a question?" Tripp asked through a mouth full of food.

"Don't talk with your mouth full, and you don't need to ask me a question to ask me a question."

"How did you get here?" Tripp asked. The other boys looked up from their plates and awaited Martin's response.

"Well, Tripp. That's quite the question," Martin replied.

CHAPTER 11

BY WAY OF A BROKEN LATCH

The alarm seemed to go off unusually early. Martin rubbed his eyes and leaned over to silence it. *4:30 a.m. on the dot.* He yawned and moved to the edge of the bed for a stretch before rising and starting his day. Opening day of hunting season only came around once a year, and he had yet to miss one since his first opening day as a young man.

He moved to the kitchen where the coffee was already brewing, thanks to the automatic timer on the percolator, poured himself a cup, and prepared a hot skillet of eggs and bacon, an opening day tradition since he moved to the cabin. Although he blessed his meal and ate quickly, there was still very much to do before he could make his trip into the woods.

He dressed in his hunting clothes—green wool bibbed overalls and a red-and-black flannel coat—and left the house to care for the dogs. He filled their food dishes and water bowls before struggling to close the kennel due to the broken latch he had yet to fix, and then started his old truck. Cold November mornings in the Northeast usually meant snow, but there was only a heavy frost this morning.

Back inside, he prepared his bag for the day. It was now almost 5:45 a.m., which meant he had to leave in the next few minutes to make the fifteen-minute ride to the property adjacent to his and be in the woods by the time the sun came up. His treasured hunting knife, a box of 30-30 bullets, and a peanut butter sandwich all got packed away in his bag. Finally, he pulled his 30-30 deer rifle from the mantle and headed to the bedroom.

"I'm off. Wish me luck," he whispered gently in her ear.

"Be safe and hurry home to me," she replied. "I have a surprise for you." Martin kissed her on the forehead and left the house—unbeknownst to him, for the very last time.

He took the bumpy dirt service road that connected his property to the property next to it. Thanks to the creek and the swampy area at its center, that property was far superior to his own for hunting. At last, Martin pulled off the road to the access point of his favorite hunting spots. Martin exited the truck and crossed the field toward the wood line.

After a short walk, Martin found himself at the ladder of his favorite tree stand. He climbed to the top and settled in for a long day in the woods. The sun crept over the horizon and warmed Martin to his core. His eyelids began to droop in the early morning light, and he began to snore.

He opened his eyes at the perfect time. The eight-point buck had caught his scent but paid him no mind as he slept.

It lowered its head and began foraging the ground for acorns. Martin scooched up in his seat, put the crosshairs of his rifle scope on the deer, and squeezed the trigger. Bang.

The buck ran away in fright. Martin was unsure what had happened. He had sighted the rifle in the day before and, after some fine tuning, declared it to be deadly accurate.

I can make that shot nine times out of ten. What happened? He climbed out of the tree stand and walked to where the buck had stood. A tuft of fur and a few droplets of blood led him to believe the buck had been hit but only wounded.

Oh no. Being an ethical hunter, the thought of the injured animal suffering made Martin sick to his stomach. His goal during the hunt was to make each shot count and dispatch the animal as quickly and painlessly as possible.

Martin followed the small blood trail for a long time before he found the animal he was seeking. The buck had wandered into the swamp to bed down and had apparently died when his adrenaline stopped driving his ailing body, but now it lay just out of reach in the muck and low water of the marsh. He slung his rifle over his shoulder and stepped into the mud as he made his way closer to his quarry.

He trod lightly across the soft earth, watching both his footing and the buck. It was slow and tedious going, but one wrong move could put him in trouble. The thin layer of ice on top broke under his feet and his shoes sank in the mud. Martin tested out his next step with his right foot, and when he was sure it was safe, he put all his weight down on it.

That's when it happened. Martin's sure footing gave way beneath him, and he sank in the mud straight up to his chest.

He started to panic. He twisted and turned, reaching for anything to grab hold of, but there was nothing. The more Martin struggled, the faster he sank. First his chest, then his neck, then his chin, until he had almost gone under entirely. *This is it,* Martin thought.

He heard crowing in the distance, followed by the sound of flapping wings. A beautiful blue bird with flowing yellow tail feathers flew in and landed in a nearby tree.

Then he heard a group of animals approaching from behind. Martin was helpless and exposed. Next he felt something cold and wet on the back of his neck, and he could hear the animals breathing. Then Toby came into view. It was the dogs! They had escaped their pen through the gate with the broken latch and tracked him to his current resting place.

"Oh, thank God. Am I glad to see you guys!"

Martin could feel the mud's hold loosen when all four sets of paws started to claw their way through the mud. All four dogs seized some piece of his jacket and began pulling and dragging Martin with all their might. When finally free from the mud, they dragged him to dry, firm ground where Martin thanked God and collected his thoughts.

"That was too close a call," Martin said to himself. "Time to call it a day." He stood up and brushed himself off before pulling out his knife to dress the deer.

First things first, he thought.

Then Martin started to feel light-headed. His head began to spin as the blue bird began to crow obnoxiously, which sent the dogs into a fury. They barked and bayed at the base of the tree, jumping and snapping at the bird.

What's happening? Martin thought. A fog rolled over his mind, and he felt as though he were floating away.

In fact, he was. Martin found himself inside a rising bubble lifting him into the air. The bubble began to spin around slowly and then faster and faster until it spun violently out of control. The last thing Martin saw was the dogs being lifted with him in a bubble of their own. Then there was only darkness.

Martin floated about inside his mind in a daze, convinced he had died. Then came a blinding light, and a deafening sound rang out in his ears. The dogs cried and howled as they licked the mud from their best friend's face. After cleaning him up the best they could, they lay down beside him, convinced he had left them.

Suddenly, Martin sat up and gasped. His lungs filled with air, and his eyes opened as he rolled over and threw up. The dogs shot to their feet and started barking and jumping uncontrollably. Martin collected himself and commanded the dogs to sit. All he wanted to do was think. At first, his thoughts were positive; he was thankful to be alive and seemingly well. Then those thankful thoughts faded as he started to gain perspective.

The first thing he noticed was that this swamp was not the same one he remembered.

"Something's not right." The dogs looked at him and started to whimper and whine. Martin was panic-stricken as he paced back and forth, trying to regain his bearings.

"You've been in this marsh, these woods, dozens of times. Figure this out!" Martin demanded of himself. He turned quickly and realized the missing piece to the puzzle was sitting right in front of him. The dogs sat there awaiting instruction, and Martin knew they could be his salvation.

"Okay, guys. Find the truck." The dogs did not budge.

"Please, find the truck!" Martin's voice trembled. Three of the dogs just sat there panting while the fourth, Toby, tilted his head. Finally, Martin began to sob and collapsed to the ground.

"The truck's not here, is it?" Martin concluded that he must have made the short trip to the afterlife. He was alone and scared. However, he would soon realize two things. One, he was, in fact, still alive. Two, he had no idea what genuine fear was.

He finally got to his feet, both angry and sad. The bitterness of things left unsaid and undone filled his mind and his heart like lead. He commanded the dogs to get up, gathered his bag and gun, and started to meander through the swamp. He wandered for hours with no set goal or destination. He walked for so long that he came to a place where the land ended, and he could go no farther. At that point, Martin just stopped and stared.

He stared into the eyes of his reflection in the swamp's murky waters for only a moment when movement in the water's reflection caught his eye. A man was standing in the high branches of a tree, just behind him. Martin was in disbelief, so he turned his gaze, and sure enough, there was a man up the tree.

"Oh, thank God!" Martin said aloud, waving his arms. But the man gave him no response. Instead, he just stood there, staring at Martin from his perch.

"Can you point me in the direction out of here? I'm lost," Martin shouted. Again, the man said nothing. Martin began to sweat.

The man, clothed in the long gray coat, looked down on Martin with a face covered by a bandana and a brown hat that he wore low over his eyes. His pointed green ears stuck out from under the hat, and when he lifted the brim, it revealed his deep purple eyes. The dogs began to growl and bare their teeth, hackles standing on end. They barked madly, lunging at the tree, jumping, and biting at the man. The Stranger—as Martin began to call him—reached into his coat and produced a small metal canister. He twisted the top of the canister and dropped it to the ground. The dogs sniffed at the canister as a thick cloud of yellow smoke burst from it. The dogs began choking and gagging. The smell burned Martin's nose and eyes from a distance, so he could not imagine the pain the dogs were suffering as the cloud enveloped them.

The Stranger then pulled a long knife from a leather sheath on his belt and flashed it at Martin. Instantly Martin shouldered his rifle and pulled the trigger, but he just heard a click. The barrel had filled with mud when he had sunk down in his swamp. With no other option, Martin turned and ran for his life. He could hear the Stranger's feet hitting the ground as he dropped from the tree in pursuit of him. Martin ran as fast as he could through puddles and over rocks, but the sound of the Stranger's footfalls still drew closer and closer. *Man, this guy is fast.* He felt the cold steel of the Stranger's blade across the side of his face. The cut was superficial but painful nonetheless.

Martin stumbled over a root and plummeted to the ground in a pile at the water's edge, where he met the gaze of his stalker. He tried to creep away as the stranger stepped forward, but it was no use. Martin had backed himself into a corner at the base of a broad tree with nowhere else to go. The pain and the fear told Martin that he was still alive, but for how much longer he couldn't tell. The Stranger took one more step forward and lifted his knife above his head. Martin clenched his eyes shut and braced for the inevitable.

It will all be over soon. Everything grew quiet, and the only sound Martin could hear was the sound of his labored breathing and his racing heartbeat. All was still and quiet inside the swamp, and Martin felt a strange and sudden peace come over him.

The Stranger thrust his knife downward, but the blow never landed. Toby, the hound, jumped through the air, grabbing the Stranger by the wrist in his powerful jaws. The Stranger let out an echoing scream as he tried to shake his hand free of Toby, but the strong dog's bite sank deeper into his arm as Toby clamped his jaws closed. The Stranger punched Toby hard in a fit of rage and sent the hound reeling. The Stranger gripped his wrist, pricking up his ears to the sound of the other dogs crashing through the swamp toward him at a rapid pace.

It was beginning to rain large, heavy drops when the other dogs arrived on the scene. The man looked down at Martin and raised a finger, waving it straight in Martin's face as if to warn him not to get comfortable and that his day would come. The Stranger fled from the dogs and disappeared into the swamp as quickly as he had appeared.

Martin breathed a sigh of relief and rushed to the side of a winded and sore Toby. He scooped up the hound, whistled for the other dogs, and bolted away at a blistering pace. His new goal was to find somewhere safe to spend the night. The storm reached its boiling point just as he broke free from the swamp's seemingly never-ending borders. With the rain stinging his face, he ran across the open countryside, scanning for any sign of shelter. Lightning flashed overhead and thunder shook the ground, but Martin continued on his course across the valley, the wind whistling in his ears.

The dogs ran ahead sniffing and searching while Martin's best tracker lay wounded in his arms. He could now see the forest in the distance and signaled the dogs, who had already started on their way toward the shelter of the trees. The rain lessened under the branches of the tall trees, but Martin continued to run. He was sure the Stranger would reappear any moment. Before long, Martin found himself running out of the forest and straight up a set of steps cut into the side of the large rock that would soon become his home. He found the cave and ducked inside, followed closely by the dogs.

Martin settled for a moment and caught his breath. He set Toby down, and the poor hound limped over to join the other dogs. Martin tried unsuccessfully to piece things together mentally. He and the dogs were tired, cold, and hungry, but the hunger would have to wait. He thought it foolish to leave the shelter of the cave, at night, in the weather, in this strange and unfamiliar place.

He stripped off his outer layer of clothes and laid them out the best he could to dry. Exhaustion crept in. He lay down with the dogs, who huddled around him for warmth, and they all drifted off to sleep. As Martin began dozing, a sense of peace calmed his heart as a whisper carried on the wind resounded in his ears.

Rest well, Martin. You are protected.

"That's my story, boys. My first day's experience and how we came to be in this strange new place," finished Martin.

CHAPTER 12

THE PLATEAU

Dylan just shook his head in frustration. He didn't mean to seem impatient, but his longing to go home and back to normal, everyday life was overwhelming. He enjoyed Martin's company, but he'd been ready to leave the valley from the moment he arrived. He longed for answers, but there were none. Every question he asked was answered with more questions.

"That still doesn't answer the question on how you got here," Dylan said finally.

"You're telling me you guys didn't experience the light and the thunderous crack?" Martin asked.

"Yes. A bright light, and a sound that made it feel like my ears would explode!" Jack replied.

"Well, there you have it." Martin said.

"Have what?" Dylan asked.

"We experienced the same things, the sound and the light. It's the signal that you're leaving our home and arriving here," Martin said.

"Right, but you came in a bubble. We didn't," Dylan said.

"Okay, so we didn't experience it the same way, but it was close," Martin responded.

"Okay, so what does that have to do with anything?" Dylan asked impatiently. "How does that explain how we got here?"

"I don't know. I'm still trying to piece this altogether too," Martin replied frankly.

"What are we going to do now?" Tripp asked.

"I have a few things to do today, and if you're all feeling up to it, I'd love to show you around. I don't think it would hurt to familiarize you with the valley while you're here. Besides that, we have more catching up to do," Martin said.

"That sounds great!" Tripp said excitedly.

"Finally, we're getting out of this cave," Jack said with a sigh.

"I have some ground rules for while we're together. When we're out and about, always stay close—no wandering or straggling. We can't risk any of you getting lost or hurt out there. Most importantly, if anything happens to me, stay with the dogs; they'll take care of you," Martin said.

Martin rallied the dogs, who were already up and raring to go.

"We have a little more than half the day left, so we need to be back before the sun starts to set. Being stuck outside at night is not ideal, to say the least." Martin ushered the boys to the mouth of the cave and started down the steps. The boys stopped on the overlook when the view of large creatures wading into the lake caught their attention.

"What's that down there in the water?" Jack asked.

"Those are sauropods," Martin replied.

"What are sauropods?" Tripp asked.

"Dinosaurs!" Dylan shouted.

"This place is the wildest environment I've ever set foot in. A wonderful, bizarre, prehistoric paradise," Martin said.

Martin led the boys down the steps and across the beach as they followed the dogs on their afternoon hike. At the edge of the tree line that encircled the Oasis, Martin stopped the boys and surveyed the fields surrounding them.

"Keep an eye out for anything that moves, boys. Everything here is either hungry or angry and looking for its next meal. Remember the rules," Martin said. After a period of watching and waiting, Martin finally deemed it safe, and they stepped out into the open.

The day was warm and still, and the sky was clear. They marched west through the field until they met with a small river.

"This river runs north to south and cuts the valley in half until it runs into the lake at the Oasis. A small crossing up here will take you across the valley toward the swamp, but we'll explore that later. There's somewhere else a little more important that I'd like to take you," Martin said, as they changed course to head north.

The boys followed Martin for a mile or two, occasionally stopping to scan their surroundings. At one point they had to duck into the tall grass as a herd of stegosauruses went stomping by just an arm's length away.

"How was that for up close and personal?" Martin joked. Jack and Dylan didn't find it very amusing.

"Whoa, that was intense," Tripp said. Martin smiled and put his arm around the youngest boy.

"You know, that's exactly what I said the first time I saw them that close. Looks like you're a chip off the old block," Martin said. "You guys okay over there?"

"They're much bigger in real life," Dylan replied. All the color had drained from his face.

"I'm all right, but maybe not so close next time," Jack answered. Martin and Tripp laughed.

They continued their course as the ground grew rocky and uneven and began to slope upward.

"Almost there," Martin said. "We'll stop at the top."

They continued to climb until the slope leveled off to a wide plateau. A river split the plateau in half before turning into a monstrous waterfall that dropped off the side of the cliff.

"The water flows from the mountain pass to this waterfall, which feeds the river at the bottom," Martin said, shouting over the roar of the falls. He pointed out that the path they were on continued climbing, narrowing as it followed the river back up the mountain.

"Don't ever go any farther up this path than here, boys," Martin warned as he stepped to the edge of the cliff. "The land beyond this point is a dangerous place."

"But the view is amazing. We're so far above the valley that we can see everything," Dylan said.

"It is a beautiful spot, but it's a dangerous place," Martin repeated. "We've now entered the domain of the Mountain Beast."

Dylan raised an eyebrow in disbelief. "The Mountain Beast?" he said with a laugh.

"Yes. Of all the things in this valley, you must be mindful of the Stranger that walks in the valley and the Mountain Beast that resides up here," Martin replied seriously.

"What is the Mountain Beast?" Tripp asked, staring up the mountain pass.

"It's an abomination of a thing. That's what it is," Martin answered. "A hulking green ogre with horns and fangs. The king of this entire valley, the Oasis included. Stay far away from here, so it has no excuse to come down into the valley. It was easier to show you where to avoid than try to explain it, but we shouldn't hang around up here much longer."

Noticing that the sun was beginning to set, Martin whistled for the dogs and led the boys back toward the Oasis. They made the few-miles trek back, and their tired legs were met with relief when they stepped out onto the beach.

"We'll get a much earlier start tomorrow, and I'll show you more of the area. But at least you're a little more familiar with your immediate surroundings," Martin said.

The boys remained silent.

Sensing that the mood had changed, Martin said encouragingly, "It's not so bad here, fellas. You'll learn your way around."

But his attempt to distract the boys from their current situation had failed.

"We don't want to learn the area," Dylan cried out. "We want to go home!"

"I know you do," Martin sympathized. "I want to go home too, or at least send you home."

"Then instead of showing us around, why don't we look for a way home?" Dylan asked.

"Don't you think I've tried?" Martin said, frustrated. "We can't just leave! In case you haven't figured it out yet, there's no exit door we can just walk through. If there was, I would have come home a long time ago, and I wouldn't have missed ten birthdays, anniversaries, and Christmases."

"So while you're here," he continued, "I think it's best that you learn your way around the area and get comfortable with your surroundings. I'll get you home; it's just going to take some time." Martin regretted losing his temper, but it had driven his point home.

When they reached the entrance to the cave, the dogs stretched out on the rug with Jack and Tripp, while Dylan and Martin continued their conversation just outside.

"I'm sorry I lost my cool, but I need you to trust me, Dyl. We can only do this together, and it makes no sense to fight over it. There are greater powers at work here, and once we have all the pieces of the puzzle, we can figure it out. Just work with me. The boys need you. I need you."

"That's the hard part," Dylan answered. "A few days ago, you were dead, and then somehow, some way, we wind up in this valley, and here you are. So yeah, I'm struggling with this, but you gotta understand—I've had no control over my own well-being or theirs since we got here. I'm just along for the ride, and I hate it!"

"I get it. I really do. But how much more proof do you need?

You need to do this, and I'm not asking. If for nothing else, do it for them." Martin gestured to the boys inside the cave.

"Who else did you think I was doing this for?" Dylan shot back. "I'm the oldest. I have to watch out for them."

"You're right; you're the oldest," Martin replied. "Be an example to them." Martin's words echoed in Dylan's ears and wrenched his heart, having heard Gram utter those exact words to him just a few days earlier. He thought long and hard before responding.

What are my choices? Trust him, because:

1. He would've come home if he could.

2. He's done nothing but look out for us since we arrived in the Oasis.

3. He's proven that he has our best interest at heart. There's a lot of proof that he loves us and cares for us.

Or, don't trust him, and be stuck here longer than I want to be.

I don't want to admit it, but I think I know the answer.

Dylan swallowed his pride and answered decisively. "You're right. I'll do it for the boys, for us. I do trust you; I do. This is just hard."

"I know it is, but if we work hard, together, we can do it. Deal?"

"Deal."

"You're not the hardest person I've ever had to negotiate with, but you certainly learned well from your mom. How is she, by the way?"

"She's good. She's on the road traveling with the band."

"I'm glad to hear that the music worked out for her. She had the gift. Except for the clarinet."

"I didn't know she ever played the clarinet."

"You wouldn't have. It happened when we were kids. She got so mad trying to learn it, she broke it in half and never spoke about it again." They laughed and joined the other boys inside.

CHAPTER 13

IN THE GARDEN

Early the following day, Martin gathered his tools and awakened the boys.

"We'll be gone most of the day, so grab whatever you'd like and let's move out."

"I don't need anything, so I'm ready when you are," Dylan replied. Tripp slipped his bag over his shoulder, while Jack shoved his slingshot into his back pocket.

Martin led the boys away from the Oasis with two goals in mind: to gather food and to show them more of the valley. Together they crossed the beach, leaving the safety of the Oasis behind them for the wide-open countryside beyond. They trekked across the fields for quite some time before arriving at their destination. A roughly built post-and-beam fence surrounded a large plot of land where the ground had been freshly turned up and an enormous garden had been planted.

Row upon row of strange-looking fruits and vegetables grew in mounds, bushes, and vines, creeping across the ground and up trellises, covering every square foot before them.

Surrounding the fence was a host of different fruit trees. Some still had buds or flowers, while others had sizeable hanging fruit fully ripe and ready to be plucked. At the foot of the trees were sweet- and bitter-smelling herbs with flowers mixed among them in bunches, attracting tiny humming-birds and butterflies.

"As I told you before, boys—we eat fresh every day," Martin said, swinging open the gate.

The aroma rising from the garden was like nothing the boys had ever smelled before, with hints of lemon, mint, peaches, pineapple, garlic, onion, and the strong smell of freshly disturbed earth. To say it was overwhelming would be an understatement, but the boys relished in the symphony of fragrances that tickled their nostrils.

Martin went to work, lifting the leaves on a largely overgrown shrub, plucking long, purple fruits that grew in bunches like bananas, and stuffing them into his bag.

"Some of these . . . oh, and these too," Martin said, thinking aloud. He moved over to one of the vined plants growing upward on a trellis and started picking what could best be described as orange grapes.

"Okay, now what?" Martin asked, looking at the boys.

"Don't ask us. We don't even know what we're looking at," Dylan joked.

"I hate vegetables," Jack grumbled. "Do I have to eat them?"

"You do—and trust me, you've never had veggies like these before," Martin added. You're going to love them. I guarantee it."

"Do they taste like candy? That's the only thing I love," Jack said.

"You're quite the goober, aren't you?" Martin said with a laugh.

"Am not. You are," Jack retorted. Martin laughed again and continued filling his bag with the strange fruits and vegetables.

Jack wandered to the corner of the fence and plopped himself down, folded his arms, and began to pout.

"Oh boy," said Dylan. "Here we go. Time for the Jack tantrum show."

"Oh, come on, Jack. He was only teasing," Tripp said.

"I'm not speaking to any of you until Martin apologizes," Jack stated.

"For what?" Martin asked.

"You called me a goober. I'm no goober!" Jack shouted.

"Whoa, partner. I didn't mean anything by it. I meant that you are quite the character with your own likes and dislikes," Martin explained kindly. "That's all. I meant no offense. Let me make it up to you."

"How? With candy?" Jack asked.

"I don't have any candy," Martin replied.

"Then how can you possibly make it up to me?"

"Let me have your slingshot."

Jack reached into his back pocket and produced his slingshot.

"Awesome! Let's have some fun, shall we?"

Martin walked to the corner of the fence, scooped up a rotten-looking melon, placed it on a fence post, and excitedly jogged back to the boys. He knelt down, scooped up a handful of small rocks from the dirt, and handed them to Jack. "Here, take these."

"What am I supposed to do with these?" Jack asked.

"Shoot them at the melon."

Jack got a devilish grin on his face. He placed a stone in the slingshot and lobbed it toward the melon, missing it by a mile. "Bummer," he said with a sigh.

"That's okay. Turn your wrist this way, draw your band back to here, and aim here," Martin said, positioning Jack and the slingshot together. "Try again."

Jack did as Martin instructed and pulled the band back again.

"That's it, boy. Take your time and slow your breathing."

Jack took a deep breath and released the stone, sending it hurtling toward the melon and knocking it from the fence post.

"Yes, that's it. Way to go, Jack!" Martin shouted. Jack was speechless.

"Okay, Tripp. Your turn, son." Martin replaced the melon and repeated the process, positioning Tripp and the slingshot together before allowing Tripp to take his shot. Tripp launched five stones through the air before he too knocked the melon down.

"That's my boy. Good job, son," Martin said. Tripp blushed.

Now it was Dylan's turn. Martin replaced the melon again and positioned Dylan and the slingshot in the same way. But no matter how closely he followed Martin's instructions, Dylan was unable to hit the melon. Dylan grew impatient, embarrassed, and disheartened all at once.

"That's all right, Dyl," Martin said encouragingly. "We'll practice some more, but I'm afraid we've run out of time right now."

"You'll get it, Dyl. I know you will," Tripp said.

"Yeah, I know you can do it," Jack added.

"What if I can't?" Dylan asked.

"You can do it. You have to slow down and feel the shot. Then you'll know when it's time to take it," Martin said.

"How will I know?" Dylan asked.

"It'll happen when the time is just right and not a minute before. You'll know it in your bones."

Martin ushered the boys out of the garden and closed the gate, totally unaware that someone nearby was watching them.

The sky was dark with the moon casting its blue light over the valley when Martin and the weary boys finally returned to the Oasis. Their slouching posture and bags under their eyes gave them away.

"You guys aren't tired already, are you?" Martin asked, seemingly disappointed.

"Hey, that was a long walk for us little guys," Jack snapped.

"Easy, Jack. You're right. I'm sorry."

Martin left the dogs in charge and returned to the valley to gather the meat for their evening meal. When he returned, he found all three boys fast asleep on the rug with the dogs alongside them.

Dinner for one this evening, Martin said to himself with a smile.

CHAPTER 14

KIDNAPPED

Journal Entry 3601

The pain is insignificant. The bones have begun to heal, and I feel my fingers will fully heal by tomorrow night. Unfortunately, my ego hurts more than the regeneration process. I took down the red behemoth, but my actions have led me to this current juncture following the encounter. Regardless of past errors, I will recover the creature's jawbones as a trophy for my efforts upon our next meeting.

Since we've escaped captivity, we've lost all track of time. It seems like we've been here for ages, but there's no way of judging. The device is valuable, but it has its flaws. I'm still only able to travel to the human world, even after all the tinkering Tiny has done to it. The concept is ingenious, but I fear it's a corrupted unit. Between the two of us, we are smart enough to reverse engi-

neer it and fix it according to our will, but where do we start? Oh, how I long to rid us of this cursed valley. Tiny is still unwell and unable to make the metamorphosis after rescuing me from the amphibian and red behemoth in the swamp. I do enjoy the company of the little blue fellow, but his pattern of speech is starting to wear on me. Tiny want this. Tiny do that. *Why must he speak in third-person narration? It's absolutely maddening.*

On top of that, the human hunter still eludes me. He is my equal in every way. I believe he will be my ultimate trophy, the true test of my abilities. He can think like me and adapt the way I can. He is perfect in every way. But alas, still, he taunts me. We've had several encounters, and he has gained and kept the upper hand at every—single—event. It's Toby, that cursed canine. He's always there with his snarling teeth. I see him for who he truly is, though it still eludes the hunter. Perhaps I could gain by having some sort of hunting companion that carried out my every command the way he does. Nonetheless, after our next encounter, he will not be the one left standing when the dust settles. My contempt for all of humanity has subsided, and I now enjoy our little game of cat and mouse.

I left the valley yesterday for the rendezvous point in the barnyard of the human world, but my crew had not yet arrived. I would venture to guess Sheamus has used the wrong coordinates. Upon my return, I had my encounter with the red behemoth.

On another note, during my reconnaissance today, I stumbled upon the hunter and those three human youths together on an afternoon patrol. Where the youths came from is beyond me, but I have devised a plan. I've watched and studied them from afar and have noted their comings and goings for quite some time. I now know that the hunter resides inside the great rock on the beach of the lake. Once my plan is executed, I will unleash the greatest weapon in my arsenal, and this entire valley will submit to me. They will be in awe of the Silverback, and with its great power, I will rule this valley until the day finally comes when we can leave it to fulfill our mission.

Alas, there's nothing else to do but wait. But I grow impatient. Day in and day out, there seems to be no end in sight to this purgatory we find ourselves in, but it matters not. I have time. I just need to keep occupied until the day does arrive. It will come. It must.

***

Vex waited until nightfall before leaving the safety of the knothole. Then he scrambled down the ladder toward the forest beyond the clearing. He searched the night sky overhead for any sign of the giant bats that patrolled the night sky and listened closely for anything moving through the tall grass or trees. He was breaking one of his primary rules of never leaving the clearing at night, but it was the only way he could execute his plan.

Quickly and silently, he scurried across the fields toward the Oasis and the residence of the human hunter. He broke free from the trees and stepped out onto the sand. Vex watched impatiently by moonlight for any sign of movement inside the human dwelling. Seeing none, he moved stealthily up the steps toward the cave and pulled a small metal canister from his coat pocket. Poking his head around the corner, he saw that the humans and dogs all slept soundly. The Stranger grinned to himself as he twisted the cap of the small canister and lobbed it inside the cave. Almost instantly, the room filled with a cloud of thick blue smoke that guaranteed no one would awaken while he was there.

He sat down on the steps and wiped the sweat from his brow. He just needed to wait until the smoke cleared before he could enter. But he hated waiting. It seemed like waiting was the only thing to do while he was stuck in this valley, which drove him mad. Once the smoke had cleared, he entered the cave calmly. *No sense in rushing now.*

The smoke had done its job, and none of the cave's inhabitants would be awake for several hours.

He planned to take all three of the boys, but with his hand in its current state of regeneration, he opted to take only the smallest. *They will worry about his safety the most.* He very carefully bound the hands and feet of the smallest boy and threw him over his shoulder. He chuckled to himself as he danced down the stairs toward the countryside beyond the Oasis.

But Vex did not realize he had made two very terrible mistakes. A pair of canine eyes were silently open and watching as he left the cave with Tripp. Toby was awake and alert but frozen in place. He couldn't move, but inside his hatred and anger for the green-skinned man grew exponentially. One day he would finish what he'd started. It was only a matter of time before the effects of the paralysis smoke would wear off. Once it did, Toby would wake the other dogs, then he would alert Martin and the boys, and they would all go after him together. Because, although the Stranger had succeeded in taking something of extreme value to the whole party, he had neglected to take something back with him—something so valuable and vital, it would once again give Martin and the dogs the upper hand. He had left behind a scent, and Toby breathed deep, letting it fill his nose.

But the Stranger's biggest mistake was one he'd made intentionally. Filled with pure hatred for Martin, he was so fixated on gaining the upper hand that he'd broken his cardinal rule of never leaving the clearing at night. Not thirty minutes after he had left the cave, Vex found himself lost in the open countryside at night.

CHAPTER 15

OVER THE EDGE

Toby stayed awake until he could rise to his feet. He let out a howl, rousing Martin, Dylan, and Jack from their resting places. The sun was up, and the countryside was already alive and bustling with activity when Jack noticed the empty spot next to him.

"Where's Tripp?" Jack asked. Sure enough, Tripp was missing.

"He wouldn't have gone out by himself, would he?" Martin asked.

"I don't know. Tripp's really independent and pigheaded for someone so small," Dylan answered.

Martin turned to Toby, who was nudging the other dogs to their feet.

"Toby, you know what to do!" Martin said. Toby's nose went straight into the air as he took in a deep breath and ran from the Oasis as fast as his stubby little legs could carry him.

"Where's he going?" Dylan asked.

"Toby will pick up the trail if there is one. And judging by his pace, there's a good one."

"And then what? Toby's too small to bring him back by himself!" said Jack.

"Toby isn't going alone, and don't judge his size against his character. That dog will surprise you. Lord knows, he still surprises me sometimes," Martin said.

Martin tucked his hatchet into his belt and grabbed his hunting rifle. Then he loaded the rifle, cocked it, and put on the safety.

"Let's go!" Martin rallied the other dogs, and they set off, hot on Toby's trail.

It took some time and doing, but Martin and the boys managed to catch up with Toby in the open countryside. He continued moving at a brisk pace, as his nose worked furiously over the hidden trail. Then, suddenly, Toby lifted his head up and bawled loudly.

Toby's cry was heard clearly across valley, and Vex's ears pricked up. The fatigue from carrying Tripp's dead weight over his shoulder melted away quickly as the thought of his pursuers flashed through his mind. He had lollygagged for too long; time was running out, and he had to act quickly if his plan were to succeed.

"He's on to something, boys," Martin said.

The four dogs took off with explosive speed, causing Martin and the boys to fall behind. They crossed the fields toward the river, where they changed their course and headed north, as they had the day before.

"Where are they taking us?" Jack asked.

"Looks like they're headed back toward the waterfall. Try to keep up," Martin called out as he quickened his pace.

They traveled up the slope toward the summit of the plateau, where they saw Tripp's small body lying motionless near the edge of the waterfall.

"There he is!" Dylan screamed.

The dogs reached him first, with Martin and the boys following at a close second. Martin took the small boy in his arms and shook him gently but firmly.

"Wake up, Tripp! Come to!" Martin shouted, while cutting the ties that bound Tripp's hands and feet. Jack and Dylan both began to tear up. Then, a moment later, Tripp opened his eyes and looked up.

"There he is," Martin said, visibly relieved. "He's awake now. Tell me what's happened, boy—why are you here?" Tripp tried to speak, but no words came.

"Thank God you're alright, son. What's going on, why are you here?" Martin repeated. Tripp again tried to speak. This time it came as a whisper. Martin leaned his ear toward the boy's mouth.

"He's . . . behind . . . you," Tripp stammered.

The Stranger had already seen them arrive and stood frozen on the path. Although he had gotten lost in the dark, he had succeeded in improvising a new plan. Martin locked eyes with him, shouldered his rifle, and pinched off a shot. But the Stranger stood fast, unflinching, as the shot whizzed

101

past him. He stood steady, staring Martin straight in the eyes. The Stranger lifted his now fully healed hand and pointed straight at Martin. The dogs edged closer, ready to spring forward and attack at Martin's command.

"Boys, stay back," Martin warned. "Whatever happens, trust the dogs!"

Martin threw his rifle to the ground and produced his hatchet.

"Let's finish this!" Martin shouted. The Stranger threw his head back and produced the most grotesque laugh any of them had ever heard.

Then Martin froze. The Mountain Beast had suddenly appeared behind the Stranger.

The mighty creature continued its path directly toward Martin and the boys, with the Stranger standing between them. On one hand, the Stranger's improvised plan had worked: Lure the hunter and the dogs up the mountain pass and let the mighty Mountain Beast do the dirty work for him. But witnessing the beast for the first time, the Stranger found himself rooted in fear.

Martin had been right. It was the thing of nightmares. It must have been twenty feet tall, with snarling fangs and dark green skin. Its massive muscular structure moved with blatant disregard for anything in its way. The scars it carried proved that even the fiercest creatures in this valley were no match for its raw brute power. Its powerful hoofed legs allowed it to move swiftly on the plateau's rocky, uneven surface, and it was closing the distance quickly.

Martin rushed toward the boys and whistled at the dogs, who broke their gaze from the Stranger and ran to their master's side. They stood their ground between the boys and the ogre making its way down the pass toward the Stranger. Then the dogs ran at the Mountain Beast with open jaws, biting at its legs and heels. The beast shrieked as it swatted the dogs away. Martin recovered his rifle and fired straight into the Ogre's chest, but it had little effect. Again Martin chambered a shot and fired, but the brute did not flinch. The bullets didn't even pierce the ogre's skin.

The ogre lifted a large rock over its head and effortlessly threw it clean across the plateau toward Martin and the boys, but it missed narrowly and crashed into the river. The Stranger had seen enough. He bolted like a coward and ran for his life down the mountain slope. The ogre managed to pull Cinder from his ankle, and he launched the dog through the air. She landed in a heap but staggered back to her feet and rejoined the fray. The dogs worked violently over the ogre's hoofs, ankles, and shins, and the beast roared in pain and anger. It punched and swatted the dogs with such force that they reeled in pain. But like a mighty wolf pack, they continued to fight valiantly to protect their human companions and keep the ogre off the plateau.

"Boys, get back to the Oasis!" Martin shouted. He again produced his hatchet and rushed toward the ogre, who had its back to them as it fought off the dogs. Martin took his hatchet and, with one great leap, landed it deep in the ogre's hamstring and held on tight. The creature spun around and let out an earth-shaking roar. As it tried to free itself of Martin's ax, the beast toppled over into the river as all four dogs sank their teeth into its legs at the same time. All together, they were washed over the side of the waterfall and plummeted toward the river below.

The boys screamed and ran for the edge. But the dogs, Martin, and the ogre had all fallen a great distance to the river below. None of them could have survived the fall, and the boys quickly realized that they were once again on their own.

CHAPTER 16

ALL ALONE

The boys were inconsolable. Sobbing uncontrollably, they huddled together for comfort. Alone again, the boys were lost and helpless in a land that was unkind to visitors. Mustering up what little courage he had left, Dylan called his cousins to their feet. Although he was still too young to fully understand it, Dylan knew in his heart that there was no time for mourning. If he had learned anything in the valley, it was that time, like everything else, was against them. They could be sad about Martin and the dogs later, but now the sun was already moving, and the clock was ticking against them.

Get them back now, cry later. We are too exposed out here, he thought.

"Okay, guys, we have to get back to the Oasis," Dylan said wiping the tears from his cheek.

"What's the point?" Tripp asked.

"Because I want to get us home alive—that's the point," Dylan retorted.

"What does the Oasis have to do with us getting home?" Tripp asked. "We don't have time to argue about this. So here it is: The Oasis is the only safe place we have here. It's kept Martin safe for all this time, and that's where all his tools and things are. So, if we can get back there, at least we have a chance for hope and survival. We need to get back now, or we're done for!" Dylan was adamant.

"You're right Dyl; I'm sorry," Tripp relented.

"It's okay," Dylan said, reaching out to put his arms around his cousins. "We have to trust one another. We can do this, but we have to work together." He held tightly to the words that Martin and Gram had spoken to him.

I will be the example. I will take care of them, and I will get us home.

The boys began their journey back down the hill toward the Oasis, where safety and shelter awaited.

"It all looks the same, doesn't it?" Jack asked as they walked through the seemingly endless meadowland.

"Remember, these fields go on for miles in all directions," said Dylan. "As long as we follow the river, we should be okay."

"I wish the dogs were here," Jack said sadly.

"Let's try to stay positive and get moving," Dylan urged. "Remember what Martin told us about being out here when it gets dark. Keep your eyes peeled for anything that moves, or anything that looks hungry. And stay together!"

The sun continued on its course across the sky, and before long, a wind picked up that blew steadily across the open fields.

"Where did this wind come from?" Jack asked. Then, suddenly, the sunshine flashed as the shadow of a large bird flew overhead.

"Wow, would you look at the size of that bird!" The giant bird of prey changed its course mid-air and began to fly back toward the boys.

"I don't like that one bit!" Tripp said.

Suddenly, the bird lowered its talons and dove straight toward the boys. The boys scattered and ran frantically in separate directions.

"Run for your lives!" Tripp shouted.

The bird missed the boys and gathered only field grass and dirt in its talons. Once more, it took to the air and swooped in toward Jack. The bird plummeted rapidly, and at the very last second, Dylan dove in and saved his cousin from being carried away.

"That was close!" Jack said.

"We have to find cover!" Dylan shouted. He leaped to his feet, grabbed Jack by the arm, and ran across the field toward Tripp, who was moving at a surprisingly fast pace. The bird circled high above them, and the boys could hear its wings beating hard against the wind. They didn't stop to look up; they just ran for all they were worth. The bird circled lower and extended its talons.

"Here it comes again!" Tripp shouted. The bird dove straight down on the group of boys.

"Everyone split!" Dylan commanded. The boys split up again, but this time continued to run in the same general direction.

They zigged and zagged across the field until they saw the tree line in close range.

"To the forest!" Dylan shouted. The bird let out a screech, and its shadow reappeared on the ground in front of them. The boys ran straight for the trees with all the strength they had left, with the beating of wings growing closer and closer.

"We're almost there—hurry!" Dylan shouted.

Just then, Dylan lost his footing, thanks to a rock hidden in the grass, and he tumbled straight down on his face. From his vulnerable position, he watched as his cousins reached the safety of the forest. Dylan felt both relief and fear. His cousins were safe, but now the giant raptor had landed between himself and the protection of the woods. It bobbed forward, adjusting its brilliant eyesight for any sign of Dylan. He lay as still as he could, but it was no good. The bird spotted him and rushed across the ground in his direction. Dylan jumped to his feet and limped as fast as he could, but he was no match for the bird's speed. It covered ground far faster than he did. Dylan tripped again in the tall grass and fell to the ground. He tried his best to crawl away, but the bird hurtled itself into the air with its talons gleaming in the sun.

Just then a giant snake leaped up and wrapped the bird tightly in its grip.

The field python had been pursuing the boys silently across the meadow, but then decided the bird was better prey. It allowed the boys to lure the bird into reach, and then it struck, grasping the bird in its powerful jaws and coiling up around it, now squeezing its bones to dust. Dylan used this opportunity to limp his way toward the forest and join his cousins, who had watched the whole series of events in disbelief.

"Let's get out of here, before the snake decides it wants to see what we taste like," Dylan said, already limping ahead.

They had already covered a great distance across the meadows before reaching the forest, and the day was almost half over. But they kept moving through the forest at a brisk pace, hoping to put distance between themselves and the open countryside.

"Can we rest here and relax for just a minute?" Dylan asked finally.

"Yes, rest your ankle," Jack said.

"I'm okay. It's only sore."

After a long silence, as they were resting on the forest floor, Dylan finally said aloud what they had all been thinking. "I wish we had more protection."

"We do!" Jack shouted. He began to stuff his pockets with rocks and acorns.

"If anything comes in range, I'll have something for it," Jack said as he launched an acorn from his slingshot. It whizzed through the air before crashing with a thud against a tree trunk.

"Great, I feel so much better now. I think it's time we move on," Tripp joked.

It was slow going helping Dylan over the large roots and rocks that covered the forest floor. Hours later, the trees finally broke, and the blinding glare from the moon on the lake met the gaze of the tired and battered travelers.

They had made it.

They walked along the beach to the rock slope and made their ascent up the rock steps. As Dylan and Tripp entered the cave, Jack stood on the overlook and took in the night-time view. *Beautiful but deadly*, Jack thought to himself before joining his cousins inside. With neither fire nor dogs, the boys huddled together for warmth, and before long, their exhaustion overtook them.

CHAPTER 19

THE TALLEST TREE IN THE FOREST

The boys awoke on their fifth day in the valley, hungry and sore.

"Well, fellas, I think we need some food, and then we should try to figure things out," Dylan said.

"I wish my dad was here," Tripp added.

"So do I," Dylan admitted. "I'm sorry we lost him, Tripp. You okay?"

"It's just not fair," Tripp cried. "First, he's gone, then I finally get to meet him, and now he's gone again!"

Dylan and Jack embraced their hurting cousin.

"Your dad is a hero. He gave himself so that we were safe," Jack said.

"I know this stinks," Dylan added, "but we need to do this the right way and survive. We can keep him in our hearts and use what he taught us to get home. Everything's going to be okay."

Tripp sighed, took a moment to compose himself, and finally rallied the best he could.

Martin's gone again, but I still have Dylan and Jack, Tripp thought. They would look out for him and take care of him now, just like they always had. Tripp remembered this and his heart swelled with pride. As difficult as it was now, he was not alone; they were together and they would succeed—for Martin, and for themselves. He swallowed hard and wiped away his tears. *Now's the time to be strong*, he told himself silently.

"First things first—what do we eat?" Jack asked.

That's Jack. Always thinking with his stomach, Tripp thought with a smile.

"The garden is too far, so I say we head back to the forest and try to find some nests and rob them of eggs," Dylan suggested.

"Simply marvelous. Lead the way," Jack said comically.

"Let's be a little more prepared today," Tripp said as he walked to the rear of the cave. He came back with three of Martin's spears, one for each of them.

As they made their way outside the cave, the boys were stunned to see all four of the dog's collars stacked neatly in a pile on the bottom step. Dylan quickly looked down the beach and saw a bear and a badger disappearing into the forest.

112

"You don't suppose those are the same animals we saw in the field a few days ago, do you?" Jack asked.

"I don't know," Dylan replied.

"Do you think they brought the collars back?" Jack asked.

"I'm not sure, but let's keep our eyes peeled today," Dylan said.

They made their way across the beach toward the forest, and before long they found a tree with many nests in its lowest branches. Dylan and Jack lifted Tripp into the air to scale the side of the tree. Tripp found the first few nests empty, but climbing a little higher proved beneficial when he saw a nest containing seven medium-sized eggs.

"Jackpot!" Tripp shouted to his cousins below.

"Great job! Line your pockets and be careful coming down," Dylan warned. Tripp did as he was instructed and cautiously made his way down.

The boys walked back to the Oasis and got to work starting a fire to cook the eggs. In hindsight had they taken the time to get one going the night before, maybe the night wouldn't have been so cold. But, at the time, the need for sleep had seemed to outweigh the need for fire.

"What a fine meal," Jack proclaimed, as the boys leaned back with full stomachs and contentment for the time being.

"Yes, sir," Tripp added.

"We need a plan," Dylan said frankly. Just then, a strange giggling sound echoed around them. All three boys tiptoed toward the mouth of the cave, and just outside, they saw a tiny blue creature with piercing black eyes.

"What is that?" Jack whispered. The tiny blue being was dancing around the mouth of the cave, giggling wildly, totally unbothered by the boys' presence.

"Wait, that's the goblin thing," Dylan said loudly. "The creature that Martin warned us about!" The tiny blue being stopped dancing and stared at them.

"Hey you, get! Get out of here!" Dylan shouted.

"Tiny not leave. Can't make Tiny!" the creature sang.

"I'm warning you!" Dylan shouted. Just then, the creature bent over, picked up a rock, and hurled it straight at Dylan, cracking him in the shoulder.

"That's it, I warned you!" Dylan shouted as he ran toward the creature.

"Tee-hee. You cannot catch Tiny. Come get Tiny," Tiny giggled as he ran down the steps.

"Well, there it goes. Good riddance," Tripp said. They watched as Tiny descended the steps and ran along the beach. Then he turned and waved the dogs' collars at them.

"Hey, you bring those back!" Tripp shouted as he ran off after Tiny.

The other two boys collected their things and made off hastily after him. Once they got through the forest and reached the plains, they did as Martin had instructed and took a minute to look around. They saw a massive wild pig foraging in the tall grass with its piglets and decided it would be best to give them plenty of space. They were also very mindful of the sky and the tall grass around them after their experience with the bird and the snake.

Tiny had wasted no time putting distance between himself and the boys. Zigging and zagging his way across the field, Tiny giggled and sang without a solitary care. Tiny was unafraid of the predators of the valley, and his sole focus was on leading the boys away from the Oasis.

"Man, this thing is fast," Dylan said, breathing hard.

"Don't lose him," Jack said. "Whatever we do, we need to keep our eyes on him."

"Let's get the collars back and then get as far away from this little blue critter as we can," Tripp added.

The boys raced after Tiny until they reached the forests surrounding the prairies. Now sheltered from the midday sun, they worked their way across the forest floor, heading in the direction of Tiny's giggles, but once more, the boys were so hyper-focused that they didn't notice a silhouette above them in the trees. Leaping silently from tree to tree, the Stranger was closing in. The boys continued their pursuit until the trees opened up into a large clearing. And there, in the middle of the clearing, stood the tallest tree in the forest.

A putrid smell filled the air.

"Do you guys smell that?" Dylan asked.

"Yes, we must be close to the swamp," Tripp responded. The boys suddenly became very aware of their surroundings as Tiny started to dance and sing once again.

"Tiny did a good job. Tiny led you all the way here. No going back now. Now you in trouble. Tee-hee!"

"I think we may have wandered into a bad place, boys." Dylan pointed at the large tree. Their gaze met with a giant knothole in the trunk of the tree, but it wasn't the hole that frightened them. It was the narrow ladder snaking up the side of the tree to the knothole. Tiny had led them straight to the Stranger's lair, and they had willingly followed him.

"I think we should leave," Dylan said abruptly. "Now."

As the boys turned to make their way back to the forest, the Stranger walked into the clearing toward them.

"What do we do?" Jack asked.

"I don't know," Tripp replied.

"We stand our ground," Dylan said as he lowered his spear into a defensive position. The Stranger rushed the boys. He leaped through the air and kicked Dylan directly in the stomach, sending the boy flying backward. Next, he grabbed Jack and tossed him overhead like a rag doll. Finally, the Stranger grabbed Tripp by his shirt collar and lifted the boy into the air with one hand. He brandished his blade for them to see, and just when he was ready to plunge it, a sound echoed in his ears that turned his blood to ice. Violent barking echoed across the valley as Toby and the other dogs, followed by Martin, came bounding into the clearing, running with wings on their heels to the boy's aid.

CHAPTER 18

SHOWDOWN

The Stranger loosened his grip on Tripp's shirt, and Tripp fell to the ground. The Stranger and Tiny both ran for the cover of the forest while the dogs pursued him. Martin, on the other hand, rushed to the side of his newly found family.

"Everyone okay?" Martin asked, scooping Tripp to his feet. The boys were dumbfounded.

"I'm okay. I just got the wind knocked out of me. Where did you—" Dylan began.

"There'll be time for that later," Martin interrupted. "Tripp, Jack, are you okay?"

"You're alive!" Tripp shouted, embracing his father violently.

"*Oof.* Okay, I'll take that to mean you're okay."

"But we saw you—" Dylan started again.

"Not now, Dyl. What about you, Jack—are you okay?"

"Yes, I'm okay, I'm really glad to see you too," Jack said, joining Tripp's embrace.

"How did you survive that fall?" Dylan asked finally.

"For crying out loud, Dylan—I don't know how I survived," Martin said, clearly impatient. "First, I felt my body get crushed against the rocks, and then there was nothing, just darkness. Then I opened my eyes, and I found myself on the riverbank. The dogs were already awake, and Toby led the way right to you."

"Well, excuse me for asking, but I don't think that was so hard to explain," Dylan replied snarkily.

Martin looked as if he'd like to strangle Dylan, and then, out of the blue, he started laughing.

"You sound just like your mother," he finally said. "I used to hate it when she said that!"

"What happened to the ogre?" Jack asked.

"He must've washed down the river," Martin said. "Either that or someone is watching out for him too. Anyhow, enough with the questions. We need to contend with our current situation," Martin continued. "The dogs are on the Stranger's trail, and today I will be rid of him for good. After that, there will be nothing left for him to grow back from," he said with a rumble of thunder in his voice and fire in his eyes.

The four of them took off after the dogs. There was no barking, baying, or howling. Instead, the dogs moved ahead silently, saving all their energy for when they caught their quarry. But when the small human hunting party caught up with their canine comrades in the swamp, it wasn't the welcome sight they'd hoped to see. Their friends lay motionless in a heap.

"No!" Martin shouted. He scanned the trees overhead for any sign of the Stranger, but he saw nothing. He shook the dogs, alive and breathing but paralyzed. The Stranger had once again poisoned them and rendered them useless.

The boys stood huddled together, awaiting instruction.

"What do we do now?" Jack asked.

"My goal was to send you back to the Oasis with them once we caught up, but now it looks like you'll have to come with me," Martin said. Neither Martin nor the boys were excited by the thought.

"He can't have gotten far," Martin said. He jogged through the marsh with the boys close behind. Seeing a small puddle ahead, Martin jumped over it and landed on the other side. The boys, however, dashed through and found themselves swept up in a snare trap by their feet, now hanging completely upside down several feet off the ground. The boys shrieked in fear and pain.

"This place is terrible. And it keeps getting worse and worse!" Jack shouted.

"Hush!" Martin commanded. The boys remained quiet while Martin tried to formulate a plan to get them down without injuring them further.

As Martin took a step back to get a broader view of how the trap worked, he put his foot straight down into a hidden claw trap that snapped shut around his ankle. He screamed in pain and collapsed to the ground. With all his might, he forced the claw trap open just enough to free his foot. Once released, he lay back and took a deep breath.

"I tell you what, boys—it's been a rough couple of days," he gasped. He tried to stand up, but when he placed his weight on his injured foot, it gave way, sending him back to the ground.

"Martin, look out!" Dylan shouted.

The Stranger had emerged from his hiding place among the bushes and was taking great strides across the marsh. In an instant, he kicked Martin square in the face, sending him rolling toward the water. The Stranger reached into his belt pocket, pulled out a canister, twisted it, and threw it beneath the boys. The blue smoke rose out of the canister toward the boys, still suspended in midair.

"Hey, leave them alone. Deal with me!" Martin shouted. His vision was blurry and his eyes watered. The Stranger's kick had landed square on his nose, and he could taste blood on his tongue.

The Stranger turned his gaze on Martin, pulled his knife from his belt, and pointed it straight at him. Martin was defenseless. He lay there in the mud with his loved ones watching as death began closing in. The smoke was starting to take effect, and the boys were feeling sick and sleepy just as the snare that held them snapped and sent them crashing to the ground. It had been designed for Martin alone and couldn't sustain the combined weight of all three boys. The claw trap had been a backup in case Martin had missed the snare. But it didn't matter. The Stranger seemed to have succeeded yet again with his planning.

The boys lay with their faces enveloped in the cloud of blue smoke that rose from the canister. They watched with heavy eyes as the Stranger moved in to finish Martin once and for all.

Martin had nowhere to turn. He waded into the water, away from the boys, to create space. The Stranger rushed him, and Martin grabbed his wrist to control the knife. As they struggled against each other's weight, Martin dealt a blow to the Stranger's face with a headbutt. As the Stranger staggered, Martin ripped the knife from his hand and tossed it into the swamp.

Now the playing field had been leveled. Before the Stranger could gain his bearings, Martin charged him again, spearing the Stranger and tackling him to the ground. Once they hit the water, the Stranger pulled Martin beneath the surface. Together they struggled to get to the surface, while also fighting to keep the upper hand. Finally Martin slipped free and kicked for the surface, but the Stranger grabbed his pant leg and pulled him back down.

Martin's lungs were starting to burn. He needed air. Martin kicked free again and broke the surface of the water, gasping. The Stranger emerged slowly and deliberately from the water, seemingly unscathed and energized.

Martin's heart sank. He was utterly spent, yet his opponent's stamina seemed limitless. Before Martin could get out the water, the Stranger sprinted forward again and grabbed his throat with both hands, lifting him out of the water. Martin struggled to break the Stranger's grip, but it was useless. Martin could feel his heart racing and his breathing getting shallow.

Without warning, Goliath, the giant bullfrog, exploded from the deep and shot out its monstrous tongue, seizing the Stranger around his waist. Their altercation in the shallows had drawn its attention, and it seized its opportunity. The Stranger released his grip on Martin to combat the frog. Martin plummeted to the ground and rolled away in the shallows as the bullfrog dragged the Stranger to his watery grave. He clawed at the muck and mire as his screams resonated through the swamp. The Stranger bellowed out one last time, as the many rows of Goliath's teeth came down on him and devoured him alive. The frog let out a loud echoing belch before returning to the depths of the dark, murky water.

Martin crawled out of the swamp and onto dry land, where he passed out from exhaustion alongside the unconscious boys.

CHAPTER 19

THE DEVICE

The four of them awoke to the dogs' tongues and hot breath on their faces. None of them knew exactly how long they'd been out. The boys massaged their ankles, trying to regain blood flow and rub the pain away, but Martin's wounds were more severe. He was almost entirely unable to walk on his ankle as the muscle swelled beneath his torn skin.

"That trap sure did a number on me," Martin said, testing his ankle gingerly.

"How are you going to get back to the Oasis with your ankle like that?" Jack asked.

"Well, fortunately for us, with the Stranger gone, we can move into his place until my leg heals up," Martin said.

"It's not that far," Dylan said, brightening.

"Precisely," Martin said with a wink.

"So, let's get moving!" Tripp said enthusiastically.

"Okay, but you boys will have to help me." The boys helped him to his feet, and after a few steps, Martin found that he could walk on his own as long as he didn't overdo it.

"You've got it now, Martin," Jack said. The boys lolly-gagged behind him as Martin limped his way back to the clearing and the tallest tree in the woods.

They found the dogs frolicking when they arrived, and the group made their way to the base of the tree.

"That looks a little daunting," Martin said, looking up the ladder.

"Let's get you up the ladder," Jack said. "You need to take some weight off that ankle."

"It's not that far up, Dad," Tripp said.

Martin shot the boy a wink at hearing "Dad" for the first time. "Not that far for us, but our fuzzy buddies will have to make do outside until we can get back to the Oasis."

"Well, up we go, I guess. Follow me to the top, and I can help pull you in," Dylan said, grabbing the first rung on the ladder.

"Be careful," Martin called out. Dylan scaled the ladder to the entry of the knothole and once inside, laid on his stomach and reached his hands out for Martin. Martin took his time climbing the ladder and found it quite awkward to maneuver the compact rungs with only one good foot. It took quite some time and doing, but he was finally able to reach the top, and Dylan was able to assist him in making the transition from the ladder to the landing. Jack and Tripp followed him closely up the ladder and rejoined him on the small platform outside the knothole in the tree.

Standing on the platform and looking in, the knothole turned out to be much larger than they expected. Martin not only had room to stand up inside; he could also stretch his arms overhead. It appeared that the Stranger had lived similarly to the way Martin lived: simply. They saw only a bed, a small table, and a large metal crate.

Martin and the boys stood around the crate, debating whether to open it or not. Finally, Martin reached down and lifted the lid.

Inside were many strange objects that neither Martin nor the boys recognized. There were different canisters, like the ones that the Stranger carried around on his belt, and an assortment of other knives. But what drew their attention the most was a pair of two small metallic disks about the size of a teacup saucer.

Jack reached in and grabbed one of the small metal disks. "What are these?"

"Hey, be careful!" Martin shouted. "We don't know what any of this is or what it does." Jack dropped the small disk to the ground, and a radiant light erupted upward from the saucer, filling the room. The light was so brilliant that they had to shield their eyes. As they adjusted to the light, they slowly lowered their hands to discover they were standing inside a hologram of the earth's solar system.

"What . . . is . . . this?" Dylan asked.

The boys began to dance around the small room, darting through the translucent planets and stars.

"Stop!" Martin shouted. The boys froze immediately. Martin lifted his hand and waved it through the air, and when he did, the hologram of planets moved back and forth in their place. He once again lifted his hand and swept it through the air, and the entire solar system began to spin around the room rapidly before slowing down and stopping with planet Earth directly in front of Martin. He reached out and touched the hologram of planet Earth. A green ring encircled it, and three green circles appeared on the floor where the boys stood.

"What is this thing?" Dylan laughed.

"This is it—the way home," Martin uttered in disbelief. *But there are only three circles, not four,* he thought, his heart sinking.

"How do you know?" Tripp asked.

"It has to be. We all encountered that bright light from the disk just before we arrived."

"How does it work?" Jack asked.

"I don't know." Martin lifted his hand again and pointed it once more at Earth. The green ring around the planet now began to shrink, and a beeping noise echoed from the device. A wild tempest arose and swirled around inside the knothole, howling loudly.

"What's happening?" Tripp shouted. He and his cousins felt a strange sensation as the cyclone of wind lifted them from the ground—the same feeling they had back in the cavern at home as they plummeted downwards to the pool.

"It's working, boys. You're going home!" Martin shouted. Not knowing how the device worked, or why only the boys got to go, he choked back his tears, preparing himself for the solitude that was coming. Tripp stretched out his arm and reached for his father.

"Come with us!" Tripp shouted.

"I can't, son—I don't know how," Martin shouted back.

"But I don't want to lose you again," Tripp shouted.

"You aren't losing me. I will always be in your heart, and we have these memories forever; no one can take that from us. Give this to Gram for me, will you?" Martin reached out and grabbed Tripp's hand, placing his wallet in the boy's palm.

"I love you, my boys! I pray that your roots grow deep and your tallest branches toward the stars!" he shouted. The room flashed with a blinding light once more, and when Martin opened his eyes, he was all alone. The boys were gone.

***

Tripp struggled to open his eyes. Jack and Dylan slowly sat up and stretched their arms.

"We're home!" Dylan shouted. He and Jack jumped to their feet and began to dance around the familiar forest, while Tripp sat and cried.

They lifted him to his feet and hugged him.

"Be happy, Tripp," said Jack. "Martin has protected us and gotten us home, just like he promised. We're home where we belong, and we know that he can survive where he is. The glorious Oasis King!"

"You're right, Jack. He was glorious," Tripp said, wiping away his tears.

"He *is* glorious," Dylan corrected.

The boys had experienced the adventure they had always wanted—and survived.

"Let's tell Grammy where we've been!" Jack shouted. The boys broke free from the forest surrounding the barnyard and sprinted across the field toward Grammy's house. They ran up the steps and threw open the door to find Grammy standing in the kitchen.

"Grammy, you'll never guess where we've been all this time!" the boys shouted over top of one another. Grammy looked up with surprise.

"Boys, boys, settle down. There's plenty of time for you to tell me all about it. But for now, why don't we settle down and have some lunch?" Grammy said.

"Haven't you missed us? We've been gone for days. Weren't you worried?" Jack asked.

"Son, you've been gone less than two hours. I've enjoyed the quiet," Gram joked.

The boys were silent for a moment. Then Tripp said, "I have something for you, Gram. A gift."

Gram knelt down and looked the boy in the eyes. "How thoughtful of you. What is it you've brought me?" Gram asked. Tripp took out Martin's wallet and placed it gently in Grammy's hand.

Gram palmed the wallet in her hand for a second before opening it. "Tripp, where did you get this?" Gram gasped, pulling a photo of Martin and Tripp's mother on their wedding day out of the worn leather wallet.

HAIL TO THE KING

Deep in the heart of the swamp, Goliath lifted herself out of the cold water and flopped herself onto the bank. She expelled her egg sack into the swamp's icy waters, let out a loud belch, put her head down, and died.

Suddenly the blade of Dylan's small pocketknife cut its way out of Goliath's stomach from the inside. A green hand emerged.

***

A few days after the boys' departure, after his ankle had started to heal, Martin left the safety of the cave to look up at the night sky, joining the great bear and badger on the overlook.

MARK DAVID PULLEN

"I appreciate everything you've done, but why couldn't I have gone?" Martin stretched out his arm and stroked the soft fur on the bear's back.

"We've done so much here already," Berrybiter, the badger, said as he stood on his hind legs. "We couldn't let you go."

"I don't understand," said Martin.

"We've created a great garden, but like the serpent last time, the Stranger has corrupted it," Adalbern, the bear, continued.

"We brought you here to protect our new paradise," said Berrybiter. "So do not fear, Martin. You will always be protected, and you will be reunited with them soon enough; you have our word."

"Protected from what? The Stranger is gone now. I saw him killed with my own eyes."

"His name is Vex. And he still lives," Adalbern replied.

The bird with brilliant yellow tail feathers fluttered down and landed on the bear's back.

"The boys followed my lead at every encounter," said the bird, Dawnfeather. "How long before we can bring them back?"

"There will be a need for them again soon enough," Adalbern answered. "The soil of our new garden is ready for planting."

"Why them—of all the people to send to me, why them?" Martin asked.

"Why not them?" Adalbern asked.

"They're children. This place isn't exactly hospitable," Martin replied.

"The relationship between a father and his son is important. No matter how far he travels away from you, the great

130

distances that separate you, as a father, would you not walk through hellfire and brimstone to bring him home safely again?" Berrybiter asked.

"Ten thousand times, if I had to," Martin answered.

"Precisely," Adalbern replied.

"I don't understand," Martin said.

"For now, you don't need to. Someday soon this will all make sense, dear Martin," Adalbern said with a yawn.

"Oh, I almost forgot," Dawnfeather said, addressing Adalbern and Berrybiter. "Your visitor awaits you at the bottom of the steps."

"Excellent," replied Adalbern. "Martin, won't you join us? You may find this little fellow to be interesting company." Martin joined the animals as they descended the steps to meet the newest guest of the Oasis.

***

The great Mountain Beast crashed against the rocks of the river. He was bruised and battered from his battle with Martin and the dogs, but the fall hurt the most. Still, the dogs did not relent. As Martin floated lifelessly facedown in the river, the dogs protected his body from the ogre with fury and rage. The dogs latched onto the ogre's flesh and clamped down. For the first time, they drew blood, and the cries of pain resonating from the ogre's throat gave them the heart to fight on.

The water continued to move swiftly underneath them, and the dogs were losing steam. Yet every time the ogre swatted them away, they would paddle back and begin their attacks all over again. He was getting too tired to keep fighting in these conditions, fighting to keep himself afloat against the current and dealing with the dogs simultaneously. The battlefield needed to change.

He grabbed for the first thing he could reach and pulled himself up onto the bank. The dogs tried to follow, but they struggled with the current and trying to drag Martin's lifeless body to safety at the same time. Something moved in the Mountain Beast's heart as it watched the dogs struggling in the water. They would drown themselves trying to keep Martin safe.

The Mountain Beast waded back into the water and scooped Martin up before tossing each dog individually up onto the bank. Finally, the beast left the river and dropped Martin on the safety of land, as the dogs closed in to inspect him. They sniffed and licked, but to no avail. Martin lay lifeless on the riverbank. The Mountain Beast watched for a bit longer before boredom settled in and he lumbered away.

He was alone and far from home. But that didn't bother him. On the contrary, new challenges and horizons awaited him here in the valley, and he embraced them. This new world was his for the taking. He was strong and mighty, and anything that dared to challenge him would come to learn just how mighty he was. He could persevere in this new, green landscape. The land was lush, fruitful, and warm. The weather up the mountain pass was always cold and snowy, and he had often longed to see the valley below. Now he had the opportunity.

He rubbed at the aches from the fall. His back hurt, and his head was still reeling, but he would make a full recovery. The pain wasn't anything he couldn't manage, but he did his best to stretch away the aches nonetheless. He headed away from the roaring river and into the valley itself.

Wandering aimlessly for food and a place to rest, he was still determined to make the land submit to his will and become the apex creature in the valley.

The very next day, he entered a beautiful clearing deep in the heart of the valley. Wildflowers grew tall and swayed in the cool breeze blowing across the meadow, and thousands of butterflies lofted into the air as his lumbering steps interrupted the tranquil ambiance of the area. Then a stirring of rage and fear filled his heart. He was not the only visitor to the valley. Another stranger walked freely among the trees and fields, and the sight of this strange thing made his blood boil.

Across the glade was a tall, steel-and-iron juggernaut shimmering in the sun. Blue and gray tiger stripe patterns of paint covered the giant metal man from head to toe. On its chest was stamped the number 001, and a tinted empty glass dome, a cockpit, sat perched between its shoulders. It stood motionless at nearly twenty feet tall, waiting for its operator to come along and bring it to life once more.

He could stand to look at it no more. The ogre charged across the glade and shoved the juggernaut. It merely swayed in place. He sniffed at it up and down, and the smell of metal and grease made him gag. He looked deep into his own reflection in the glass dome and let out a roar so loud and mighty that the glass fogged and cracked. Still the juggernaut did not move. Feeling he had proved his dominance to the lifeless machine, he gave it another good shove, and the Juggernaut toppled over and shook the ground when it landed.

As he turned to exit the glade, a whirring sound accompanied by a loud thud made him stop in his tracks. The juggernaut had come to life, picked itself up, and was standing once more. To see this enraged the Mountain Beast, and he released a deafening roar, spraying saliva and baring his fangs. The juggernaut let out a loud hissing noise as the glass dome lifted to reveal the pilot of the machine. He remembered the puny green man from the plateau. His deep, purple eyes taunted the Mountain Beast from afar as he grinned at him smugly from his perch, challenging him to combat. Seeing the green-skinned man again angered the Mountain Beast, and he charged at him from across the clearing.

They collided and went to work against each other as a cloud of butterflies rose into the air, fogging their vision. The juggernaut was made entirely of steel and other heavy metals, yet it was surprisingly fast and light on its feet. It evaded every punch and kick thrown by the ogre with effortless ease. It delivered blow after blow to the Mountain Beast and received none in return. The ogre was bruised and bloodied by the time he finally got a grip on the juggernaut. He embraced the iron giant around the midsection, launched it into the air with one swift twisting motion, and sent it flying across the glade.

The juggernaut struggled to all fours as the Mountain Beast began delivering powerful blows to its back with his hooves. A swift kick to the side sent the juggernaut flying again. This time it recovered and got to its feet. The ogre charged again. The juggernaut dropped to the ground and swept the Ogre off his feet. It stood up and seized the ogre by the ears, raising him into the air. The Ogre looked deep into the green-skinned man's purple eyes and began to struggle before the juggernaut delivered the final blow.

The juggernaut dropped the great Mountain Beast to the ground, and he lay there unconscious. Not dead, but badly defeated. It spun on its heels and strolled out of the glade, leaving the Mountain Beast behind.

"All hail the king," Vex said aloud to himself. Now that the machine had been thoroughly tested, there were more important matters at hand.

ACKNOWLEDGMENTS

T hanks to Marlene Bagnull, Barbara Haley, Dave Lambert, Mindy Aramouni, Rich Ellis, Shirley Merritt, Barbara Beck, Heidi Vertrees, Violet Batejan, Payton Teeples, W. Terry Whalin, and Amanda Rooker. My dear friends, your knowledge of this craft and priceless feedback made this book possible.

ABOUT THE AUTHOR

Mark David Pullen is an author of middle-grade and young adult fiction. He resides in upstate New York with his wife, two children, and their crazy pup Toby, where they spend much of their time in the great outdoors. Mark always had a vivid imagination as a child and used it as a tool to escape the daily struggles and trials of growing up, but his calling to write did not manifest itself until his mid-twenties. His goal is to provide his readers with stories of action, adventure, and exhilarating danger, all while pointing them toward the love of Christ.

A free ebook edition is available with the purchase of this book.

To claim your free ebook edition:

1. Visit MorganJamesBOGO.com
2. Sign your name CLEARLY in the space
3. Complete the form and submit a photo of the entire copyright page
4. You or your friend can download the ebook to your preferred device

Print & Digital Together Forever.

Snap a photo   Free ebook   Read anywhere

CPSIA information can be obtained
at www.ICGtesting.com
Printed in the USA
LVHW030952270223
740291LV00004B/16

9 781631 959615